Energized

Energized—The Making of a Teenage Superhero
Copyright © 2019 by Tim Tweedie

Credits

Cover art & illustrations © Tim Tweedie

All rights reserved. No part of this work may be reproduced or used in any form by any means—graphic, electronic, or mechanical including photocopying, without the written permission of the author.

This is a work of fiction. Names, characters, and incidents are either the product of the author's imagination or used fictitiously. Otherwise, any resemblance to actual events, locations or persons, living or dead, is coincidental.

LCN
ISBN 978-1-945539-33-6

Energized

The Making of a Teenage Superhero

Tim Tweedie

Dunecrest Press

Dedication

This book is dedicated to my amazing wife for the support and assistance in the editing of my books. Also, to my six inspirational grandchildren who bring me much delight.

Contents

Chapter	1	How Could This Happen?	1
Chapter	2	The Power of Light	19
Chapter	3	A Day at the Zoo	34
Chapter	4	The Covert Volunteer	51
Chapter	5	A Part-Time Job	67
Chapter	6	Bullies and Crisis	81
Chapter	7	Wake and More Work	98
Chapter	8	The Window Man & Brace	115
Chapter	9	The Satellite	127
Chapter	10	FBI and Space Mountain	142
Chapter	11	Followed and a Freighter	156
Chapter	12	Gary, Ferrell, and Gerard	169
Chapter	13	A New Hero and Tsunami	184
Chapter	14	Seeking Answers	197
Epilogue			207

Chapter One

How Could This Happen?

Did you ever wake up in the middle of the night and sit up quickly because you had just realized that something very important had happened to you that would affect the rest of your life? At first your thoughts are confused because you know if you lie back down you might forget why you're so concerned.

This happened to me less than six weeks ago. My life and the lives of those close to me changed direction and there was no turning back.

In the beginning I started to do unusual things that made me wonder what was going on, but I didn't feel much different about myself than I usually did. I was just a sixteen-year old active boy who enjoyed a good time. I didn't understand fully the responsibilities that would be part of my new and amazing, but sometimes scary, altered world.

This is my story, the start of my journey that I share with you just as it happened. Even now I find it difficult to believe that this story is about me.

"Tyler! You said you'd play football with us. Now get up and go long," yelled Jonathan, Tyler's seventeen-year-old triplet cousin.

Tyler rolled over on his beach blanket and slowly stood up.

"I sure do love getting a good tan! Makes me feel healthier," he replied taking a moment to stretch.

"This is your birthday beach party and you said you wanted us all to play football in the sand, so come on!" shouted Tyler's younger sister, Kensie.

Tyler quickly sprinted toward his other cousins, Mikaia and Nicholas, who were already throwing the ball back and forth along the wet sand as the waves occasionally brushed their bare feet.

"Another beautiful day at the beach," he shouted, as he abruptly cut in front of Jonathan to intercept the throw from Nicholas.

"Why do you keep intercepting the football that's thrown to me?" an annoyed Jonathan asked.

Tyler laughed and replied, "Because you're older and the fastest one out here besides me. I just wanted to make a statement."

"Okay, you've proved your point. Now throw the ball and let's pick teams," Jonathan replied.

Tyler signaled for Mikaia to go long. Then he threw a ball that seemed to float forever before dropping way beyond Mikaia's reach.

"The idea is to let me catch the ball, Tyler," yelled Mikaia.

"Sorry, I was just warming up."

"Let's make it boys against girls!" suggested Jonathan.

"You must be kidding!" Kensie exclaimed.

Jonathan, realizing that his suggestion was not particularly popular, replied, "Yes, just kidding. Then how about me and Nicholas against you, Tyler, and Mikaia?"

"Now that could be a game," Kensie replied as Mikaia tossed the ball to her.

Tyler's parents, Matt and Christina, had driven in from Century City to pick up Tyler's cousins from their home in Torrance so they could attend his birthday party at Redondo Beach. They had dropped off the cousins at the beach for most of the day. They had planned to return with Tyler and Kensie's younger sister, Sydney, along with a special lunch. The beach was one of Tyler's favorite spots. Actually, any place it was sunny drew Tyler.

After Jonathan caught his pass, Nicholas raised his arms and yelled "touchdown!" while Jonathan did a little dance in the surf.

"I'm sure glad you chose beach football for your party and not your favorite sport, basketball," said Mikaia when she realized her team was seven points behind.

"The beach basketball courts are always crowded. Besides I wanted the shorter ones among us to have a chance at scoring," Tyler replied.

"Thanks for the short joke but remember we're both on your team now and unless we score more points, Nicholas and Jonathan are going to get the game winning prize your parents brought."

Tyler thought for a moment as Nicolas prepared to kick off to them.

"That's the exact incentive I needed!" he shouted as he ran forward to catch the football which had dropped in front of him.

Within a moment he had dodged Jonathan and run past Nicholas to the imaginary end zone. Both Kensie and Mikaia decided they'd do a little dance too, just to let Nicholas and Jonathan know their team wasn't going to take any guff from them.

"You know, Tyler, it's almost unfair to have you on a team. You already know that no one in our school can outrun you; probably no one in our town," said Jonathan

"Yeah, I'm fast but I'm sure many guys in town can beat me."

"Hey, since we're all tied up, why don't we get our surf boards ready? asked Kensie.

"Mom and Dad said we could head out when they returned and my watch tells me they should be here any minute. Besides I'm tired of watching those guys at the south end of the beach catch those nice waves."

"Good idea," replied Nicholas, "except there does seem to be a stronger than normal undertow. I've noticed it moving the surfers as they wait for waves."

"We'll just have to be extra careful and stay close to our boards. Besides, those kids up the beach just swam beyond the surf without any problem," replied Jonathan.

"I see that the lifeguard is keeping an eye on them although he seems to be eating his lunch now," added Mikaia.

"Watching the lifeguard, Mikaia? I bet you have. He's kind of cute, isn't he?" asked Kensie.

"I was just saying…"

"We know, Mikaia. You were just checking out that flock of seagulls right behind him," Jonathan said.

As everyone but Mikaia laughed, something in the water in front of the lifeguard tower caught Tyler's eye. There appeared to be a lot of splashing just beyond the surf. Obviously, the lifeguard had failed to notice it, but Tyler picked up the sounds of someone panicking.

"There is trouble out there and the lifeguard doesn't see it!" Tyler yelled.

He grabbed his surf board and quickly was halfway up the beach. As he ran, he yelled towards the lifeguard tower, but the guard had climbed down for a moment probably to get the rest of his lunch.

Tyler hit the water on his surf board while Nicholas and Jonathan were just grabbing theirs. Several others, including the boy's mother, were screaming to get the lifeguard's attention. Tyler shot through the surf and in an instant pulled the thrashing young boy from the riptide current even before the lifeguard had had a chance to figure out what was happening.

Holding the boy on his board, Tyler quickly paddled them both in through the surf and onto the shore. The lifeguard raced to meet them and carefully checked the little boy who was coughing up the saltwater he had swallowed.

"I'm sure glad you were around!" exclaimed the lifeguard as he placed the boy into his frantic mother's arms.

"I just dropped out of the tower for a moment to finish my lunch and then this happens. Actually, you saved the boy from drowning and me from having to live with that!"

"I'm just glad I noticed. It all happened so fast," Tyler replied.

"Speaking of fast, I've never seen anyone move as fast as you. Is there a motor on your surfboard?" the lifeguard asked, trying to calm down the situation with a little humor.

"Not that I know of," replied Tyler starting back down the beach after he met Nicholas and Jonathan returning with their boards from the water.

Tyler heard Jonathan say, "Greased lightning!"

"What is that all about?" asked Tyler walking towards his parents who had just arrived carrying a couple of picnic baskets followed by his younger sister, Sydney.

"That's your new name. You saw and heard things we didn't and were in and out of the ocean before I had a chance to toss on my beach shoes!"

Before the boys arrived at the picnic site, Kensie had filled her parents in on the amazing event.

"We hear you saved a boy from the under-tow. Great job and quick thinking, Tyler!" said Tyler's father, Matt.

"I was just lucky to see what was happening. It all seemed like slow motion to me. Right place at the right time, I guess. Anyway, what did you bring for lunch?"

"Actually," replied Tyler's mother, Christina, "we picked up some Kentucky Fried Chicken and Pizza along with chips, sodas, and chocolate chip cookies.

We figured you'd prefer that to any sandwiches I could make."

"I really like your sandwiches," replied Tyler, "but for a beach party the chicken and pizza are great!"

As Kensie, Nicholas, Jonathan, Mikaia, and Sydney attacked the lunch, Matt and Christina knew that they had brought the right combination of food for Tyler's beach birthday.

"That was an awesome party we had yesterday," Tyler said when he and his family stepped out of their van upon their arrival home after church.

"We're glad you and your cousins had such a great time," his dad replied.

"Would you mind if Kensie and I ran up to the McDonalds on Pico for lunch? They've just put this chicken, bacon, and olive sandwich on their menu and I hear it's great," stated Tyler.

"I haven't prepared anything for lunch yet, so if that's what you'd like to do, it's fine with me," replied his mom.

"Great! You do want to come don't you Kensie?"

"Sure, but I want to change first, especially if we're going to run."

"Oh, that was just a figure of speech, but we could get some running in if you'd like."

"Then I'll put on my running clothes and we can make a loop around the park first. That should wake up our appetites!"

"Be sure to put some suntan lotion on before you go, especially if you're going to run around the park." said Matt.

"It's bright and you'll be running right towards the sun when you head west on Pico."

"Gotcha, Dad," replied Kensie.

Even though Kensie was two years younger than Tyler, they'd always been a team. Tyler made sure she was included in most of the things an older brother did. Besides she always seemed to be ready for just about anything. If Tyler took it easy, she could keep up with him on a four-mile run around the park.

Since Sydney was several years younger than Kensie and still in Middle School, Tyler and Kensie had spent more time together recently. At home, Kensie and Sydney did a lot of "girl" things together and big brother Tyler, much to his relief, was rarely included.

"How about a second loop," suggested Kensie.

"You are in great shape today. But since we're just a few blocks from that chicken, bacon, and olive sandwich I've been thinking about, let's just head to McDonalds."

Kensie smiled and nodded.

"That sun sure is bright," noted Kensie, adjusting her cap as they jogged down Pico towards McDonalds.

"Yeah, but there seems to be something going on where Overland comes in," said Tyler speeding up.

"What is it? I don't see anything."

"It looks like a bad accident to me, Kensie, and I think I need to check it out! See you up there!" Tyler yelled as he quickly disappeared into the sunlight.

Tyler ran several blocks in seconds and arrived at the intersection where he saw three cars tangled up with one on top of another, burning. People were starting to gather but were cautious about getting too close due to the smoke and flames.

A man and a woman standing near Tyler were telling someone how they were lucky to have gotten out of their car before it caught on fire.

Inside the lower car, and through the smoke, Tyler spotted two people in the front seat who were apparently trapped due to their crushed roof. Almost as a reflex action, Tyler found himself next to the lower car straining to push the burning top car off. Soon that car flipped over and tumbled to the other side. Tyler quickly grabbed the passenger side door handle and tried to open this accordion shaped door that was stuck in the car frame. Within a moment or two, the door came loose as the flames enveloped the rear of the car and headed towards the passengers.

As several men approached, Tyler picked up the woman on the passenger's side and handed her to the closest man who immediately rushed away from the flames. Then Tyler reached over to the driver's side, yanked away the steering wheel that had pinned the driver, and pulled him out. The other men carried him to safety.

Then Tyler stepped back into the crowd just as the flames engulfed the entire car as a fire engine as well an ambulance appeared.

"Wow, Tyler," Kensie said as she pushed through the crowd and appeared next to him.

"How'd you push that car off the top?"

Tyler was silent for a moment as he watched the firemen and medics move into action.

"I really don't know. It's all sort of a blur to me. One moment I sensed something was wrong and then my legs started moving."

"Your legs just started moving? You seemed to float, no fly towards the accident. I saw you push the car off from a distance and only arrived when you moved back into the crowd. How'd you do that? I knew you were fast but that…"

Again, Tyler just stood staring as though he were completely detached from the scene.

"I think I want to get away. Let's move back to the McDonalds we just passed."

As they moved away from the crowd, they heard someone yell out, "There he is. He's the one who saved them!"

Tyler started running.

"That sure is a great burger," said Tyler. "I think I'll have another."

Kensie took a bite of hers, shook her head and said, "Tyler, we need to talk about this. You're acting like nothing happened, but it did. What's going on?"

"I really don't know and it scares me," he replied. "Over the last few weeks everything I do seems to be getting easier. I can hear and see things before anyone else, like on the beach today and the accident just now. I go to throw a short pass and the football just takes off on me. I see someone that needs help and suddenly I'm moving to help. I can't explain it. How could I push a car off another?"

"I don't know what to say," Kensie replied. "I had noticed lately that you seem to excel at everything, even simple things like knowing the answer to something I've never heard of before. I kept thinking you were just going through a growing phase, you know, from childhood to young adult or something that guys do. Even when we ran, you never got winded and seemed to strain to hold back so we could run together."

"So, you think there is something going on with me?"

"I certainly do after today. You just saved two people from a pile of burning cars."

"Maybe I should see a doctor. Maybe I have some kind of disease or crazy gene in my chromosomes."

"I really don't know. I suppose you should talk to Mom and Dad about this."

Tyler pulled another fry from his tray and stared at it.

"It's weird...my mind is telling me where this potato came from and I don't even want to know!"

Taking the final bite of her burger and quickly chewing and swallowing it, she asked, "Where is it from?"

"Why do you want to know?"

"Just wanted to check something."

"Idaho," he replied as he tossed it into his mouth.

"See, even your mind knows things you've probably never even thought about...How's that?"

"If I knew that, I'd probably know why I feel like I can lift a car...even two cars. Maybe I should talk to Mom and Dad and see a doctor."

"Or maybe you should spend some time trying to figure out what is actually happening to you."

"What do you mean?"

"Try different things to see what happens. You know, test yourself and check out the how and whys...like how fast you can run and how much you can actually lift. And when you ran down Pico today why did you seem to be flying above the ground?"

"Maybe I got bitten by a mutant spider, or dropped in on Mom and Dad from another planet when I was a baby. I often wake up at night thinking about things like that."

"You're just being silly now."

"Then you explain it to me."

"Well, you seem to know things you don't even want to know. So why can't you figure this out?" Kensie asked.

"I have no idea. Maybe I'm afraid to find out. But I think you're right, I need to try some things out before I worry Mom and Dad with all this."

Late that afternoon, just as the sun was nearing the western horizon, Tyler left for another jog. Both he and Kensie had pledged not to say anything to their parents about what had happened, at least for now. The noise of the day had dissipated. Tyler saw only a couple of other runners as he approached the park and golf course. He figured that instead of running around the park and golf course he'd run through them. Fewer people would be there than along the sidewalks and roads.

He cut across the first tee checking for anyone who might see him. He could see to the furthest part of the course. Only a tree or two blocked part of his vision. The depth and clarity of his sight surprised him. Even in the twilight he seemed to have some kind of night vision.

His feet seemed to find exactly the right spot to land which helped him to run even faster. Soon he was dodging trees as they appeared before him. Nearing the eastern side of the course he circled around and ran directly west into the setting sun. His speed increased and the trees he passed became a blur. He glanced towards the road and realized he'd just passed several speeding cars. He began to slow down. He was totally confused.

"Clear your mind," he ordered himself.

In an instant his confidence was back.

"Jump, go ahead and jump," came an inner voice.

"Why?" he replied.

His mind responded, *"You know why."*

Tyler thought he did know why, but he had to find out for sure. He decided to jump towards the setting sun. He crouched down and threw his arms up as he jumped, springing forward. He ended up above the trees flying through the sky from the third tee to its distant green before landing gently. Dismay was his only emotion. He had done the impossible again.

"Try it again," returned the voice.

So, Tyler turned around to jump back to the third tee. Even though the sun had set he could clearly make out the tee markers. Again, he took the position and thrust himself into the sky only this time barely reaching the tree tops and flying only half the distance before gently floating down.

"That was unexpected," he thought. *"But I can really jump, and I float like a heavy cloud, but I float!"*

He decided to jog back home. He needed time to think. How could he run so fast and jump so high? Why did he sometimes do it faster and further than other times? Finally, what's making him change from a typical boy to someone who can do things beyond normal human capabilities? With these concerns no wonder he had trouble sleeping.

As he jogged through the dark park and came out into the lights of Los Angeles, he felt his legs strengthen as he sped up. This sudden burst of speed startled him as he consciously told himself to slow down. Again, Tyler wondered what was happening.

Passing a rock garden display on a corner of an apartment building complex he abruptly stopped. Among the various plants were arranged several large boulders obviously placed there by a bulldozer. He soon found himself in the garden picking up the largest of them. He felt as though he had only lifted his backpack from his bedroom floor. He quickly dropped the rock to the ground.

"How could this happen? Why was this happening? What was all this doing to me?" he wondered.

A moment later, as he entered the house, Kensie greeted him with a cheery. "You're back! How was your run?"

There was a pause as he sat on a bench near the door to take off his running shoes.

"Actually," said Kensie, "you look like you saw a ghost, what happened?"

"Hey, Tyler," called out his mother. "We'll have dinner in fifteen if you want to shower."

"Thanks, Mom. I think I will," he replied as he signaled for Kensie to follow him to his room.

"I can't believe what you're telling me! You're becoming Super Boy or something. Are you sure we have the same parents?"

"Yes, I'm sure. I even helped Mom change your diapers when you were born."

"Let's just not go there. Remember, we both changed Sydney's. You are my brother, but you seem to be becoming different from a normal brother."

"It sure looks that way. It's so weird. For a moment I feel so powerful, then fearful because I don't understand what's happening to me!"

"It may be time to tell Mom and Dad," said Kensie.

Tyler didn't appear to agree as he looked down shaking his head.

"What if they want to put me in a special school or let some researcher run a bunch of tests on me?"

"I don't think they'd ever let that happen."

"Then what if they had no choice, like if someone saw me?"

"I don't know, Tyler. This is new to me too. Do you feel like you can control these things that happen, and keep them a secret?" she asked

"Right now, unless I consciously tell myself not to do something, my body moves forward. I see an accident or problem and I'm moving before I have a chance to fully evaluate the situation. I'm told to run, jump, or pick something up and I'll do it unless I stop myself."

"So, you do have control?"

"If I make an effort," sighed Tyler.

"Then maybe we should sleep on this and talk more about it tomorrow," suggested Kensie.

"Yeah, if I don't jump out of bed and run after a fire truck tonight."

Chapter Two

The Power of Light

Tyler's dad was up early, reading the morning paper as he often did before he drove to work. His mom had just walked over to the kitchen sink as Tyler entered and gathered some cereal, rolls and fruit for a quick Monday morning breakfast. Following him were Kensie and Sydney, both still in their pajamas. Tyler sat down near his dad, while Sydney took a glass of orange juice that Mom had just poured and sat down next to him. Tyler glanced up to see Kensie staring at him.

"I did get some sleep and I didn't hear any fire trucks," he mentioned.

"I didn't hear any either," replied Mom not fully understanding what Tyler was saying to Kensie.

"This is sure something," Dad said, gently shaking the paper while looking at Tyler and Kensie.

"There was a big accident just down Pico yesterday about the time you two were out running.

It says three cars got tangled up and some kid threw one car off another, yanked open the door on the crushed car below, and pulled the two people who were trapped inside out just before it burst into flames.

Tyler glanced over at Kensie and slightly shook his head, "No."

"Oh, that's what all that commotion was about down the street. We were at Mc Donald's about that time working on that new burger I wanted to try and paid little attention to it," replied Tyler.

"Well, from what I'm reading you missed a virtual miracle. A man took a video of everything with his phone and there's a photo that shows the back of the person who did it..."

Kensie looked again at Tyler who suddenly appeared pale.

"But there is an awful lot of smoke so it's hard to see him clearly, the article says, even from other videos people took."

Tyler let out a long breath he'd been holding.

"It says that the hero just disappeared into the crowd. No one seems to know his name but several people were able to give partial descriptions of him to the police when they arrived."

"That must have been something," Mom said. "I'm just glad no one was badly hurt."

"Did they really say this mystery boy was a hero?" Kensie asked as Tyler bumped her arm.

"According to the witnesses it would have taken several strong men to flip the car off and probably the Jaws of Life to cut open that squashed passenger door. If he hadn't been there, those two passengers would have been...let's say, toast. That sounds like a hero to me."

"Hey, Kensie, change and I'll walk you to school. We haven't got much time," suggested Tyler.

"Now tell me again why you have to go to school today and so early?" Mom asked.

"Good question," said Dad, his eyes still glued to the paper.

"Aren't there three weeks left of summer?"

"True. We're both on our high school's 'Planning Committee to Welcome Freshman.' Kensie is representing the new freshmen and I am one of the junior class representatives."

"That's right! I remember now. You did say something about that committee to me last week. I just forgot to tell Christina about it."

"Then when will you be back?" asked Mom.

"Probably around noon," Kensie replied.

"I'll call you if we're going to be later," added Tyler as they both hurried out of the kitchen.

"I thought for a moment I was going to get caught!" said Tyler, on the way to the high school.

They traveled a couple of blocks and turned east on West Olympic Boulevard before deciding to cross at the intersection with Century Boulevard. They could see an ambulance in the distance and hear its annoying siren heading towards them. Pausing at the intersection, they waited for the green light before crossing. The light quickly changed and they hurried across.

"That ambulance is really moving," noted Tyler.

"It's signaling to make a left turn up Century. I hope it slows down. That's a sharp turn."

"I don't think the driver is paying attention or he doesn't see the turn," said Kensie.

They both started to move faster. If the ambulance made too sharp a turn, it could roll over right where they were standing.

"He's going way too fast Kensie! Let's run!" shouted Tyler.

He instantly moved a hundred feet beyond the intersection. Sure enough, the driver had completely misjudged the turn and was attempting to make it at an unacceptable speed.

A second or two passed before the ambulance flipped over and bounced, spinning through the air towards where Kensie was running. Tyler sprang back to her and threw her out of the way. He was right where the vehicle was going to hit. He threw up his hands as though to protect himself and dug in his legs making himself a human cushion to lighten the blow the ambulance was about to take. As it hit him, he rolled, slowing both its speed and spin. A moment later it stopped.

A frightened Kensie realized that Tyler had been hit. She ran towards the ambulance as the two medics, who apparently were not badly hurt, climbed out the driver's side door which was now facing up. She saw Tyler pinned underneath. But a grunt or two later the ambulance jerked up a couple of feet and Tyler emerged. Kensie ran over and hugged him.

"Are you all right?" she screamed.

To Kensie it seemed like several minutes of silence before Tyler, with his torn shirt and a small dirty scrape on his face, replied.

"I think so, but I really didn't think I was going to make it."

Both of the emergency personnel were sitting down, leaning against the ambulance. They looked confused but all right. Several cars had stopped as the traffic began to back up.

Tyler, who had regained his composure, turned to Kensie.

"Quick! Let's get out of here before people realize what happened and start asking questions."

She nodded and held on to him as they made their way up the street towards the school.

"I thought you were crushed under that thing! The ambulance fell right on you, right where I was standing. You saved me."

"Well, I wasn't going to let it hit you. I figured I had a better chance of surviving than you...and I did."

"Are you sure you're okay?"

"I'm fine, I think. But I am upset about my shirt. I'd planned to wear this one the first day of school and now look at it!"

"How, did you survive that? You should be spread all over the pavement!"

"Like I said before, I don't know. But I did learn something else about myself from this."

"What?"

"I think I'm nearly indestructible."

For a moment Kensie stepped away from him and studied his face.

"Tyler, what's happening to you? Now I'm really getting worried."

Tyler approached her and took her hands in his.

"Kensie, don't worry. I feel fine and it's not like I have a fatal disease. I don't know what has happened to me, but I do know that unless it stops soon, my life will be changed."

"What are you going to tell Mom and Dad?"

"I'm not sure. I need some time to think. Many things keep flying through my mind that I don't understand. I need to be alone for a while and think.

Go on ahead to the meeting. Tell them I'll make the next one. I'll meet you at home in a couple of hours."

"Where are you going?"

"Wherever my mind takes me," Tyler replied as he turned and headed west down Olympic.

The pier above completely blocked the sun.

A block or two later he climbed onto a bus that was heading towards the beach. Twenty minutes later he exited at one of the beach souvenir shops and bought a tee shirt that read, 'I'm from Sunny California,' and threw his old one in a recycle can. He worked his way down the hill onto the Santa Monica Pier and took the stairs down to the long and wide stretch of beach that cradled the Pacific Ocean. After staring at the water, he sat down against one of the many pier pilings. The pier above completely blocked the sun. It was almost dark, yet the sunlight was warm and bright an arm's reach away.

"God, are you trying to tell me something? What do you want me to do?" he asked.

He knew that over the last few weeks he'd been feeling different...more alive, aware, and energetic.

Earlier he had chalked that up to becoming a young man, a natural occurrence like having his voice deepen. Yeah, he was becoming more athletically competitive, if not dominant. He figured that was part of it too...but now this entire Superman stuff! Speed, unbelievable strength, indestructibility, urges to move into dangerous situations, these were much more than just maturation.

He knew that the last two days had completely changed him. What's with this saving drowning people, or overturning burning cars? And now even saving his sister by catching a tumbling ambulance? Was he just the most unlucky guy in the world or simply in the right, or wrong place at the right or wrong time?

As he sat in the shade, he felt his body begin to relax. The moisture from the breaking waves began cooling him down. He even felt like he could take a nap. After all, he hadn't slept much the night before.

He closed his eyes and readjusted to a more comfortable position against the pier piling with both his legs in the sun. He lay still and began to doze off. Suddenly his eyes opened. Taking a nap was the last thing he wanted to do! What had he done, taken an energy booster drink and swallowed an overdose of caffeine? Why did he feel like he wanted to run all the way to Malibu Beach?

"What's happening to me!" he shouted as he pulled his legs up against his chest and hugged them.

In a moment his body relaxed. He sat up and looked out at the sun baked beach, then at the dark waves that were breaking in front of him under the pier. He slowly pushed his arm from the shade into the sun and held it there. After a few seconds his body began to tense up. His mind became more alert. His body was saying, *"at least run to Muscle Beach!"*

Tyler began to smile as he rolled out into the sunlight and looked up with his eyes closed. Just as he figured, he soon felt like he had had a second energy drink.

He rolled back into the shade and felt his adrenalin rush weaken.

"The sun!" he thought. *"My body must be a large solar cell or something. It gives me all kinds of energy and stimulates my entire body and mind!"*

Tyler began a quick review of his last few days. Each time he did something amazing, it was a bright sunny day. It was a sunny day when he threw the football so far on the beach, and when he rescued the drowning swimmer. It was sunny when he tossed a car off another and ripped off a jammed-in car door to rescue people.

But what about his amazingly fast run through the golf course and park yesterday in the late afternoon? Before twilight he ran fast, but as the sun began to set, he slowed down. Then when he jumped into the setting sun, he jumped high and far. And, when he jumped back, away from the setting sun, he only floated half as far.

When he found himself in the middle of the darkened park, he was able to run, but not as fast. Yet, when he emerged and saw all the city lights, he sped up.

"*Sun and light, depending on the amount, seem to charge me up,*" he thought.

"*When there is less, I can still do amazing things, but I don't have as much strength. My body absorbs sun and light and seems to store some for the dark but allows me less energy. Sun and light rays stimulate me as they would a solar cell that produces energy, then electricity. I'm a dynamo!*"

His excitement soon turned to worry as his mind filled with even more questions.

"Why me? How long will this last? Will I get even stronger and more powers? What am I supposed to do now and how do I live with this?"

Tyler told himself to stop. He really couldn't handle any more unknowns today. He still had to deal with the answers he'd just discovered.

Fortunately, Tyler arrived home just as Kensie was coming up the street.

"Where did you go today?" she asked.

He paused, and then he asked, "First, how did the committee meeting go?"

"Fine, everyone was there but you. I told them that something had come up but you would be at the next one. Now where did you go?"

"To the beach."

"To what beach?"

"The Santa Monica Beach and pier."

"Well, what did you do?"

"I bought this neat T-shirt to replace the one I tore."

"You know what I mean."

"I sat under the pier and thought. I needed time to think."

"Then what did you find out?"

"To save some time, I found out that I'm like a solar cell that gets its energy from light beams, especially the sun. In the dark I'm only semi-super, but when I'm hit by bright light or the sun I'm charged up and ready to do almost anything."

Kensie paused because she needed time to process what Tyler had told her.

"This is hard to believe. Why you? And how long will this last?"

"And those, Kensie, are several of the many questions I still need to figure out. Until that time let's just keep this our secret."

In the middle of the night something woke Tyler again. He sat up and looked around the room. Then he spotted it. Shining through his curtains was a full moon. It looked like a giant search light in the sky. He felt a rush of adrenalin. Somehow, he knew he needed to dress and go outside.

As he quietly shut the front door, he moved to where he could see the moon clearly. It seemed to be pulling at him. Like a moth he was being drawn to its light. He started running towards it, knowing full well that he'd never reach it. Then his mind told him to jump. He remembered the long jump he'd made into the setting sun the day before so he obliged. Up he went, straight towards the moon as he gathered tremendous speed.

He felt the wind blowing on his face and body so he leaned forward into the Superman position and he sped up even more. He was flying, but straight at the moon. What was making him fly just at the moon?

Why couldn't he break free and gently float down like he had yesterday?

"*Think! Think!*" he told himself.

Then it hit him. He gets power from the light, especially the sun light. Street lights gave him power too, but now it was the moon.

He was flying straight toward the moon.

"*I need a bright light from somewhere and quick before I'm up too high and can't breathe.*"

He searched below and saw a football stadium completely lit up. As soon as he focused on it, he changed directions and headed towards it. He let out the deep breath that he had been holding.

"Now what? I'm flying at a tremendous speed, but how, why, and where is it taking me?"

As he approached downtown Los Angeles, he caught a glimpse of a large highway billboard advertising some new movie release. At that very moment his body turned and headed for the sign.

"Wow! Every time I focus on a new light source I move towards it. Light not only gives me energy but it also attracts me and keeps me flying! It's my direction finder."

With that thought he searched for the park and golf course near his home. If he could find a lesser light source maybe that would slow his energy and his speed and let him land without crashing!

There it was, that one bright light that they left on by the golf clubhouse.

"Focus," he told himself.

Again, he changed direction and his speed decreased...a lot. He concentrated on the putting green next to the light and his direction shifted slightly while he slowed down and then dropped to his feet. His left foot settled into one of the putting holes

"Got to watch that sort of thing when I'm landing," he thought as he lifted it from the cup.

He stood for several minutes on the darkened green. He was excited but scared. He could fly! And he could control his direction by focusing on various light sources. They also gave him energy, to varying degrees, to do the other amazing things he had recently discovered. He felt as if he had been transformed into a full-fledged superhuman. But how was this happening? And why was it happening to him?

"What am I supposed to do with this new ability? And who do I tell and what do I say? This not only changes my life but also those around me, especially those who know my powers."

He found himself walking back to his home and quietly entering his bedroom.

Chapter Three

A Day at the Zoo

The following day Tyler's dad, Matt, and Uncle Nathan had planned to meet at the Los Angeles Zoo.

As a kid Tyler had loved the zoo and when Kensie and Sydney were born their family continued to go often, usually with their cousins. The zoo was located off highway 5 in Griffith Park. The Gene Autry National Center of the American West and The Railroad Museum were located there too.

"When are we leaving, Dad?" Kensie asked.

"Just after you finish breakfast. It's about a thirty-minute drive and opens at 10:00 a.m."

"I can't wait to see our cousins again," Sydney added.

"Me too!" interjected Tyler as he walked into the kitchen.

"You're up later than usual and you still look sleepy," observed his mom.

Tyler reached up and stretched and said, "I had a lot of thinking to do, and it seems my mind wants to do it in the middle of the night."

"That's my pattern sometimes too," said Dad.

"Then maybe it's inherited," suggested Kensie.

"If that's the case probably half of Los Angeles is related to us," added Dad.

Tyler smiled and sat down just as a plate with two large pancakes appeared before him.

"Thanks, Mom. Your pancakes are always fine!"

"I'm glad you still enjoy them, but what in the world are you thinking about that keeps you awake?"

Tyler noticed Kensie look over at him obviously to see what he was going to say.

"You know the usual things."

"Like what?" she replied having the curiosity of most moms.

Tyler fidgeted for a second, then plunged a large piece of pancake into his mouth.

"Jussst a mmiinute, Mom."

He needed a moment to think. Should he tell them what was really keeping him awake, or should he continue to put it off? Kensie knew most everything except what he'd learned last night. He could trust her to keep his secret, but he felt that she wanted him to tell. Maybe they could figure out why this was happening to him. Maybe there was something in their family history, or medical records that would at least explain part of it. Yet, if there were some strange things in their family history, his parents would have told them by now.

They often talked about their European and Asian ancestry mix. He did know a lot more about his European side. Maybe there was something on his mother's Asian side. But he still wasn't sure.

"You know, being a Junior in high school and playing in two sports along with taking two AP classes. You know, the usual stuff," Tyler finally answered.

"I guess I'd be a little worried about a schedule like that too," Mom replied as she dropped the last pancake onto his plate.

When Tyler walked back to his room to get his baseball cap, Kensie stopped him.

"You went out last night," she said.

"How'd you know?"

"I got up to use the restroom and heard you come back in."

"Yeah, I couldn't sleep. The full moon woke me up."

"And then what?"

"What do you mean?"

"I mean I know something must have happened by the way you're acting this morning, so..."

"Since we're getting ready to leave, I'll be brief. I found out that I can fly too."

"You can what?" exclaimed Kensie.

"Shush! I discovered that light, any kind of light, not only gives me my energy, but also lifts me up and pulls me towards it."

"How high and how fast did you go?"

"Very high and very fast!"

"This is crazy!"

"Don't you think I know that? I'm just not sure why or what I'm supposed to do about it."

"Maybe now you'll tell Mom and Dad."

"Hey kids, let's load up," called their dad.

"We still need to talk."

"I know, Kensie. I'll fill you in later."

In the zoo parking lot, they met up with Uncle Nathan, Aunt Cathy, and their cousins. Everyone was excited to visit the zoo again.

"I hear they've got this new Rhino Experience," said Nicholas as they started towards the front entrance."

"What is that all about?" Sydney asked.

"I think they get them to do some tricks, things Rhinos don't usually cooperate with," replied Nicholas.

"That should be interesting," said Jonathan, "like trying to get you to clean your room."

"Now that really would be a trick," Nicholas replied with a smile as he ran up to the ticket counter to be first in line.

"Usually you're the first in line, Tyler," mentioned Mikaia.

"Let's just say I'm having a 'take it easy' day,"

Jonathan looked around at him. "He must be sick."

Nicholas took a closer look and replied, "Yep, he's sick," as they all began to laugh.

"Okay, whose turn is it to buy the churros?" asked Sydney.

"I think its Mikaia's turn," said Jonathan. "I did it last year."

"Do you still have the receipt?" asked Kensie.

"Yes, on my desk next to the vanilla ice cream cone I didn't finish that day."

"Sounds to me like he's telling the truth," replied Kensie with a big smile.

"Then I'll do it," said Tyler.

"Great, thanks," said Nicholas. "I'd like my usual three."

"If you don't want to end up as lunch for the hyenas, you'll enjoy the one you're going to get," replied Tyler.

Pausing for a moment, Nicholas replied, "Then I'm sure I'll enjoy the free one that you're going to buy."

"And I know I have another fifty yards before the churro shack. That should give me time to find enough loose change along the path to get you that one," replied Tyler as they walked past the souvenir shops beyond the entrance.

Each of the cousins, armed with a warm churro, marched east towards the Rhino Encounter area. There was a canopied riser just above it which made for great viewing. A small crowd had gathered to watch the two large beasts that the trainers were putting through their paces.

"I sure wouldn't want to be in the jungle at night and wake up one of those," said Jonathan.

"Even with their size they can run almost as fast as a horse," said Matt.

"Yeah, but once they get close to you, I don't think they're going to just tickle you with that massive, sharp horn," replied Nicholas.

"I think I'd rather see the chimpanzees anyway," stated Mikaia. "They're a lot safer and they act like little clowns."

"Me too," agreed Sydney.

"I'm game," replied Kensie as she, Sydney, and Mikaia headed up the path to the chimpanzee compound.

"Okay, we'll come too as long as we get to visit the tigers after that. They're probably the meanest and most unpredictable animal here," said Jonathan.

"After the chimps I think we adults will head up past the giraffes to the restaurant and save a couple of tables for an early lunch," mentioned Nathan.

"Fine with us," said Tyler as the group turned and headed further up the path.

"Okay, everyone line up for a picture," said Christina as she removed her cell phone from her purse.

"We'll see if we can't make those chimps in the background seem like part of the family."

"Then Nicholas, you'd better get up there behind us too," said Jonathan and everyone laughed.

"And you'd better not stand too close to the tiger railing. The zoo has a scheduled feeding right about now," returned Nicholas as they all laughed again.

Everyone seemed to want to take a picture of the group. Cell phones appeared from everywhere.

"Okay, okay, enough with the pictures," said Matt.

"We'll meet you at the restaurant."

"The cousins headed further up the paths that led to the hippo, bear, and tiger enclosures.

"There's my friends," said Jonathan as he held open his arms to the tigers as if to hug them.

Then he reached for Nicholas's shoulder.

"Just want to let you know, friends, that I've brought you your lunch."

Nicholas reached out to grab Jonathan's shoulder and said, "If I go, you go. That way the tigers will get a second course."

"That's enough," said Mikaia who was still smiling. "We're not paid to feed them. Besides the two of you would probably give them gas."

Everyone laughed at that scenario as Kensie pulled out her cell phone.

"Now let's get someone to take a picture of us," she said looking around for a likely candidate.

"Excuse me sir," said Nicholas to a young man walking near him. "Would you mind taking our picture?"

"Sure, if you take one of me and my girlfriend afterwards."

Nicholas spotted the attractive young lady and instantly agreed.

"Back up to the railing so I can get you all in. I think I can even get that tiger just below you in the frame."

The cousins were so focused on the camera that they didn't notice a child's stroller gaining speed down the path to their left. Jonathan was standing on the left side of the group with Nicholas and Tyler on the right and the girls in between.

A women's voice suddenly cried out, "My child! My child!"

As the cousins looked to their left, Jonathan had but a second to react as he became the stroller's target. He took two quick steps forward trying to catch it. He managed to stop it and push it back from the railing, but in doing so the force and weight of the fast-moving stroller threw him up and back over the protective bars of the pit. He toppled down twenty feet into the enclosure.

Everyone turned in disbelief and looked down. Tyler thought that the impossible had just happened.

Jonathan was moving as he lay on the ground. The tiger, who had just received an unexpected visitor, looked confused. Then he began to move forward, probably thinking he'd just been given his dinner which usually arrived about this time.

"Jonathan!" shouted Nicholas. "Are you all right?"

Jonathan moaned as he pushed himself up to a sitting position.

"I think so, but everything's spinning."

"We've got to find a way to get him out of there!" yelled Mikaia. "Someone needs to run for help."

Several people, who had been drawn to the tiger enclosure by the commotion, pulled out their cell phones. The tiger was methodically crouching down with his eyes fixed on Jonathan. His muscles were rippling as he tensed up preparing to pounce.

"Jonathan, you've got to run or something..." shouted Kensie.

Before she had finished, Tyler appeared below in the enclosure. He was standing still just in front of Jonathan staring directly at the tiger. The tiger stood up and took a step back. He was obviously shaken by Tyler's sudden appearance.

A moment later Nicholas lowered a garden hose he'd noticed in a nearby planter down the side of the enclosure after wrapping it around the railing.

"Jonathan, climb the hose," he whispered.

"Jonathan," Tyler said softly while still staring at the Tiger. "You need to try and climb out. I would help you but I shouldn't take my eyes off the tiger."

"Yeah, I'll try," he replied as he slowly stood up and moved the four steps towards the dangling hose.

Jonathan took hold of the hose, pulled himself off the ground, and then set his feet against the enclosure wall. The tiger's eyes followed him. Part of his meal was getting away. He resumed his previous position, focusing on Tyler and preparing to pounce.

In a flash, the tiger cleared the fifteen feet to Tyler. At that same moment Tyler, equally as fast, jumped and turned to his left. A gasp could be heard from the people above as they realized Tyler literally 'had the tiger by the tail'. He swung the tiger around two times letting it fly through the air about twenty feet before it hit a wall and slid across the dirt surface of the enclosure. The tiger immediately took shelter in one of the caves.

Tyler took hold of the hose and followed Jonathan climbing out of the pit.

There was total silence, and then loud applause as Tyler appeared above the railing. Jonathan was surrounded by Nicholas, Kensie, and Mikaia who all wanted to see if he was hurt.

"I'm fine," Jonathan said, "thanks to Nicholas and Tyler. But I'm sure I'll be plenty sore tomorrow. By the way, Nicholas, the tigers weren't my friends and I did almost become their lunch."

As Tyler checked on Jonathan, everyone's attention turned to him.

"How'd you do that?" asked Nicholas.

"How could you jump that fast into a deep tiger's pit, and then throw him around like a stuffed doll?"

"I guess I just reacted. Something had to be done and Jonathan wasn't in a position to get out."

"We knew you were fast, Tyler," said Mikaia, "but tossing a dangerous tiger through the air?"

"Must have been adrenaline, you know like when a single man lifts a car off someone trapped below it...that sort of thing."

Everyone was trying to get close to the conversation to hear what Tyler was saying.

"Step back everyone," came a voice from the crowd as three men approached.

One was dressed like an animal trainer, another man carried a tranquilizing rifle, and the third looked like some kind of medical specialist.

"Is everyone all right here?" asked the medical specialist.

"Yeah, I'm the one who was knocked into the enclosure and I'm okay." said Jonathan. "Probably have a few bruises tomorrow."

A lady nearby exclaimed, "Yes, he's the one who stopped my stroller and child from falling into the tiger area. He saved my son. He's a hero!"

As she spoke the specialist quickly examined Jonathan.

"Who's the one who jumped into the compound?" asked the trainer.

"He is," said Kensie, pointing to Tyler.

"Well young man, you're awful lucky that the tiger didn't harm you! Amazingly you saved your friend and yourself. We have cameras on all the animal compounds and we saw what happened when the stroller knocked your friend in. How in the world did you do what you did? It takes three of us to even lift a sedated tiger."

"I certainly hope your tiger is all right," Tyler replied.

"He seems to be, but I'll check him out later. So, how'd you do that?" the trainer asked.

Tyler looked around and saw every eye on him. "Like I said, it must have been the adrenaline."

He was hesitant about saying anything further. In fact, he didn't know what else he should say.

"If so, I've certainly never seen anything like that before," replied the trainer.

Jonathan and Tyler signed a couple of papers for the zoo stating that they were all right and the cousins all headed back towards the restaurant.

"How did you jump into the tiger's compound so fast and then swing him by his tail?" Mikaia asked.

"I just reacted," Tyler said shrugging his shoulders.

Nicholas, who seemed a little frustrated, looked at Tyler and said, "Come on! It's got to be more than that!"

Walking next to Tyler, Kensie caught his eye and softly mouthed, "Maybe you should tell them."

After thinking about what Kensie had suggested, he whispered back, "Okay, then you tell them, but it has to be a secret."

Kensie stopped on the path and everyone else stopped with her.

"Actually," said Kensie, "Tyler has changed a lot lately, not as a person but in what he can physically and mentally do."

"We thought something was going on. The last few times we've been with you it's like you've been super energized or something," replied Jonathan.

"I will tell you more with Tyler's permission," said Kensie, "if you agree that what we're about to confide in you will be kept a secret, a secret that each of you must promise to never share, unless Tyler lets you."

The cousins and Sydney gathered around Kensie and Tyler. Each said that they'd keep whatever they heard a secret.

"Tyler has gradually gained superhuman powers," informed Kensie.

"What kind of powers?" Jonathan asked. At that point Tyler decided to speak.

"Actually, I can run so fast you'd have trouble seeing me. I can jump as high as I want and lift just about any weight. So far, I'm virtually indestructible. I can be hit by a speeding car and walk away."

"What?" gasped Sydney. "You mean you're like Superman?"

"You did see me grab a tiger by his tail and throw him twenty feet didn't you? I actually could have tossed him over the trees if I wanted to."

"This sounds impossible," stated Mikaia. "We sort of knew something was happening to you but this?"

"Oh," said Kensie, "Tyler can also fly!"

"Do you have wings or something?" asked Jonathan.

"No," replied Tyler.

He couldn't help but smile. The idea of flying with wings had never occurred to him.

"I get my power from the sun and other light. I seem to absorb their energy. And if I focus on a light source it rapidly pulls me towards it along the ground or into the sky!"

"How, why, did this happen to you?" asked Nicholas.

"That's something I still need to figure out, along with what I'm supposed to do with these powers."

"You do like lying in the sun," suggested Sydney.

"And would rather be outside than inside," added Jonathan.

"Yeah, I do feel that my body's similar to a large solar cell that's able to absorb and store large amounts of light energy. That's why I'm twice as powerful during the day and, depending on the light source, not quite as strong at night."

"Could you fly right now?" asked a curious Nicholas.

"Of course, all I have to do is focus on a light source and I'm gone."

"Will you do it now?" an impatient Jonathan asked.

Kensie stepped in.

"No! He shouldn't. Tyler's concerned about what other people would do or expect from him if they knew his powers. He must be very careful."

Nicholas, who had been in deep thought, added, "Then that must have been you on that news video a couple of days ago at the accident near your home. You tossed over a car and saved two people!"

"Kensie and I were out for a run and, yeah, that was me."

"And then the next day, also near your home, some ambulance drivers said on TV that they'd rolled over at an intersection and been saved by someone who miraculously caught them!" added Mikaia.

"Oh, that too. We were on our way to school for a meeting," said Tyler.

"You're already a hero!" replied Nicholas, "and you're lucky that no one had a good look at you today if you want to keep your secret!"

"Yes, I'm trying to avoid the spotlight."

"We'd better meet our parents soon or they might think something is wrong," suggested Kensie.

"But something is wrong, or at least very exciting," said Jonathan. "Do your parents know?"

"No, they don't. I didn't want to worry them, yet," replied Tyler.

"Then are we going to tell our parents about the tiger?" asked Sydney.

"I don't think we can," said Kensie, "without giving away Tyler's situation."

"But they're going to find out at some point," inserted Mikaia.

"True," replied Tyler, "and they will, as soon as I figure out a few more things."

As the cousins approached the café above the giraffe compound, they found their parents sitting at two tables which had a great view of both the giraffes and the zoo.

"Glad you could finally make it," said Nathan as they approached.

Just then a man walking by with a young boy in tow looked over at Tyler and said, "Hey, nice job with that tiger back there!"

Matt looked up and asked, "What was that all about?"

"Oh," Mikaia said quickly, "that's the reason we took so long."

Everyone was anxiously waiting for her to finish, not sure what she would say about her brother.

"Tyler just helped with one of the tiger tricks."

"That was nice," said Christina. "Good job."

Chapter Four

The Covert Volunteer

That night Tyler went to bed early. He needed time to think. He rolled around for an hour or two then finally drifted off to sleep. Suddenly, he woke up. He found himself sitting up in bed once more. He glanced towards his window curtain because he thought that the moon had awakened him, but it wasn't visible. Then something told him to go outside. At first, he tried to ignore the thought, but it continued. Finally, he gave in, got dressed, and snuck out.

Once outside he felt the same sensation he had when he first flew.

"Why is this happening?" He thought.

Then it became so clear...homework! If he was going to use his powers, he needed to practice. He needed to have confidence in them, so he could control them instead being controlled by them. So, he caught sight of a distant street light and jumped. In a second or two he was almost face to face with that light. He quickly focused on the lights on the top floor of a distant building. He flew toward them at great speed.

"*Now look up!*" he thought. "*Find a bright star.*"

He looked to the north and found what he knew would be there...the North Star. He flew toward the star at a forty-five-degree angle and was able to control his flight! He just needed to be aware of the light sources around him, decide which direction he wanted to go, and then focus on a light in that direction. As he practiced flying, he approached some of the brightest lights possible to keep his energy levels up.

After a while, he looked for a place to land and found a single dull light to slow him down. On the top of one of the highest buildings in downtown Los Angeles he spotted a light that flickered above the roof doorway where he gently landed.

Looking over the city he could clearly see the Santa Monica Pier miles away. Even his sight at night was getting stronger. Though he'd practiced for an hour he wasn't tired. He felt elated, strong, and energized. He sensed he had the power and ability to do anything. He felt invincible.

As he watched the city move below, he wondered what life would be like now that he had these powers. Did he even want what he'd been given? Did he want to be watched, evaluated, scrutinize by everyone and especially by law enforcement agencies? He knew the agencies would watch him, even try to use him, but is that what he wanted? They would find out sooner or later. Maybe he should escape to some place less populated where he could just be himself. Northern Nevada, the Dakotas, even Alaska would keep him out of the public eye. Yet, he was still just a young man. What would he do there?

It's strange, he thought, that his mind could focus so fast, even bring up information he didn't know he knew. It seemed like someone had plugged a memory chip into his brain loaded with everything he needed to know as well as unnecessary information. But he couldn't figure out exactly why he had these powers, how long they would last, or even what he was supposed to do?

Below him he heard the scream of several fire engines. He glanced east and detected smoke rising from an apartment building. As he focused, he could see flames and an ambulance approaching. Tyler had a sudden urge to dive down and help.

He concentrated and stopped the urge. What was he becoming, a cliché?

He'd seen superheroes like Superman, Batman, and Spiderman do the same thing a hundred times. Off the high building they'd go! They were just Marvel Comic book characters, cartoons from someone's imagination. He was a real boy, a person. This was not make-believe.

"If I dive down, am I supposed to begin a career working for the Police Commissioner, or be on the Mayor's Special Force Unit? Do I really want to expose myself so everyone knows I'm around?

"But what if I could have helped and read in tomorrow's paper that someone was killed, someone I might have been able to save? Do I always hide my powers, not use them for good, the gifts that for some reason God has allowed me to have?"

Again, Tyler had the same urge, except now his mind told him that someone was in immediate trouble.

"Great!" he thought and jumped, using the flames as his light source.

Instantly he saw the problem. The complex was on fire. The many firemen below were moving people out with some using the extended ladders. But apparently the ladders didn't reach to the roof where a trapped man and women were huddled near the edge, waving and shouting. Tyler landed a few feet behind them.

The man turned and for a moment just stared at Tyler.

"How did you . . . ? Then you're trapped too, Son. We're trying to get the firemen's attention but it's no use. The ladders are too short."

"Sir, I can help, if you trust me," Tyler said calmly.

When the woman turned towards Tyler, he could tell she was in total panic mode.

"How can you help?" she screamed. "We're going to die!"

"Just trust me and do as I say."

"What's a kid going to do, fly?" she screamed.

"Something like that," he calmly replied. "You'll both need to grab hold of me."

"We what? For what reason?" yelled the man.

"So I can take you down."

"How? The staircases are on fire! Are you going to jump?" he asked.

"Yes, but I have a plan...you'll have to trust me."

"Why?" the lady yelled.

"Because you have no other choice, do you?" Tyler asked.

"He's right!" yelled the man. "We have to trust him!"

"Then each of you stand at my side so I can put my arms around you and you can hold on to me."

Tyler knew he was taking a chance. He'd never picked anything up and flown with it. But what choice did he have besides leaving the couple on the roof?

They approached Tyler apprehensively and took a position on either side of him. He curled his arms around them and searched for the strongest light source. He noticed a search light a few blocks away probably flooding the sky for a new car dealership. He jumped and off the side of the building they went. He dropped a few feet then quickly gained altitude and speed as he moved towards the light.

At first the woman screamed hysterically, and then there was silence. Within a few seconds Tyler's legs absorbed the rather hard landing next to the search light.

"How in the world did you do that?" the man asked.

"I'm just glad you're both all right," he said as he found another light source and jumped.

Tyler was soon home and in bed. Should he have helped? But then if he hadn't, the couple would have been lost to the fire. He really didn't have a choice. Now he realized that he must use his powers for something good. What exactly would that be?

The next morning when Tyler got up to shower, he was stopped in the hallway by Kensie.

"You were out last night, weren't you?" she asked.

"Did you hear me come in again?"

"No, I didn't, but this was a good clue," she replied as she handed him the morning paper.

"Couple Saved from Fire and Death by Flying Stranger," the headlines said.

"And you think that was me?"

"Duh, who else?" she replied.

"I was just getting in some practice when I noticed this couple stuck on the roof of a burning building. What was I supposed to do?"

"You did the right thing. Did anyone besides the couple get a good look at you?"

"No, not that I know of. I even dropped them off a few blocks away from all the commotion."

"The couple said that they would have died if you hadn't come along. Many reporters don't believe them, but no one can explain how they survived."

"Good! Then it's a big mystery and I go on with my life," replied Tyler as he headed towards the bathroom.

"But something's going to happen soon!" Kensie called after him.

"What's going to happen soon?" asked Christina as Kensie walked into the kitchen with the paper.

"Oh, you heard me talking to Tyler?"

"Just the portion I mentioned, that echoed down the hall."

"The morning paper had so many things in it that I was just pointing out that virtually anything could happen."

"That seems to be the case recently. Two people were saved from a burning building last night by a boy who flew!"

"Where did you see that?" Kensie asked.

"Oh," replied her mother, "I was just scanning through the news on my phone. The couple are either delusional from their near-death experience or we have a super boy in the area."

"It's probably the delusional thing," mentioned Kensie as she laid the paper on the table.

While Tyler showered, he tried to think of how he could use his powers. What he'd done so far was good, but it only helped a few people. Finding a way to help many people all at once might be a better use of his time. But how would he do that? Then he remembered the news articles he'd read over the last year. Every major disaster or problem suddenly scrolled like a video through his mind.

"Those are tragedies that affected many people, but what could I have done?"

He recalled a bus loaded with people in Arizona that had rolled over on a bridge. It was hanging precariously over the edge of a deep river canyon, held only by a small cable that had wrapped around it. The people couldn't get out. A tow truck was on its way, but arrived too late. The bus and everyone in it fell into the canyon below. If he had known, he might have been able to save everyone.

"That kind of thing," he thought.

"Maybe I could fly in a shipping container full of food or medical supplies to some disaster area that has been cut off. But then a helicopter could do

that...not if there weren't any available. I'd have to know about such catastrophes right when they happened and what the people needed most? How could I do that?

"Living in the Los Angeles area where many news and disaster support agencies are located would be a benefit. Maybe I should volunteer and link up with one of them. The deal would be that if I helped, I would stay out of the news. I could be a covert superhero no hiding in caves or ice palaces...no masks to wear or autographs to sign. I could still be just me.

"School! How would I do that? I couldn't just receive a phone call and run out of my U.S. History class. But I would be making history. Maybe that would help my grade. But then some people would know, like my teachers and the Principal. But if I was home taught it wouldn't be a problem. But then, I wouldn't be with my friends, or play sports, or go to the Junior Prom, all the neat stuff like that."

Tyler finally figured it was about time he talked to his parents. He had enough information about himself and his new powers. He still didn't know how this had happened, but he'd just figured out the why. Maybe he was given these powers to not only help a few people, but also to help many people in major catastrophes which could make a major difference!

Tyler felt that tonight would be the right time to share what he knew. Again, he was concerned. What would his parents say? What would they do? How would they react to having a son who could fly and grab a tiger by the tail and throw him across the ground? This would change their lives, too!

Tyler spent his day as he normally would. He and Kensie took a run around the park and then drove golf balls at the golf range.

Upon arriving home, Kensie gave some sisterly attention to Sydney by helping her wash and blow dry her hair.

Tyler and Kensie had arranged to go with their mother and Sydney to Costco and Wal-Mart to gather some school supplies and look for birthday gifts for their cousins. After that they returned home to complete some chores they'd been assigned.

It was also Tyler's turn to make dinner. He actually liked to cook. He, Kensie, and Sydney had helped their mother so often that they were all capable of planning and creating meals for the family. He had decided to go light with a Cobb salad and pea soup. His 'green team' as he called it. He'd also picked up an apple pie and some French bread from Costco which he would warm with a butter and garlic spread.

Yet, this evening would be different. As they finished the apple pie Tyler knew it was time to speak.

"Dad, Mom, I have something to share with you. What I'm going to tell you is hard to believe. I've been dealing with it for some time trying to figure things out by myself. It's nothing bad, but it is changing my life."

He had his parents' complete attention. He had already told Kensie and Sydney and now he was going to tell his parents.

"Over the last few weeks I have been gradually changing. In the last several days I've changed a lot."

"How have you changed?" asked his mom.

"Please let me finish what I need to say. You'll understand then."

"I've somehow received some superhuman powers. There are things I can do which possibly make me the strongest person on earth."

"What are you talking about?" Matt asked. "You seem perfectly fine to us. Maybe you're a bit stressed. Some rest and less worry about school and everything is probably what you need."

"That's not what has stressed me lately. Let me describe what I can do so you'll understand," said Tyler. "Remember the news article a few days ago about the person who threw a car off another, then ripped off a door to save two people, and nobody knew who it was? It was me."

"What are you talking about?" his dad asked.

"Just wait a second, please. And Mom," Tyler continued, "the news you found on your phone about a young man saving a couple from the top of a burning building in downtown LA? That was also me."

"But how could you do that?" asked his mom. "We didn't even know you were out that night."

"Kensie did, and she's known about this for some time. I told Sydney more recently."

"Kensie, is all this true?" asked their mom.

"Yes," replied Kensie, "all that and more. Tyler now has many super powers."

Their dad and mom just sat, as if in a daze. They seemed to be trying to process what they'd just been told.

Finally, Dad asked, "What kinds of powers do you have?"

"Yeah," yelled Sydney. "Can you fly faster than a bullet?"

"Probably, but as far as powers are concerned, just about all of them. When I run, I'm a blur. I can lift just about anything. I can see and hear things others can't. My mind gives me information I've never learned."

Still not believing what she'd just heard, Mom asked, "How did this happen to you?"

"That's one of the few things I've not figured out. We don't have any superheroes in our family, do we?" he asked.

"No, from my family history research, you'd be the only one," replied his dad.

"I don't know anyone in my family either," added Mom.

"Then I still don't know."

"You haven't been sick or hit by a bus or anything?" asked Mom.

Tyler couldn't help but smile.

"No, Mom. However, I did catch a flying ambulance the other day off Olympic and Century."

"That was you too?" asked his dad

"Yeah, I guess Kensie and I happened to be in the right place at the right time."

"I'm still not sure about..."

Before his mom had finished, Tyler picked up the chair she was sitting on and lifted her high in the air.

"Tyler, what are you doing?" she yelled as she grabbed hold of the chair.

"Just giving you a simple demonstration," Tyler said as he gradually put her down.

"Wow!" exclaimed his dad. "That was either some kind of trick or Tyler is what he says he is."

"Take my word for it! It's all true!" stated Kensie.

The talk continued for some time. Tyler explained what had happened to him over the last few weeks and his reaction. He told them why he hadn't said anything to them before this. For a long time, he just wasn't sure what was happening. He didn't want to worry them. It wasn't until everything sped up that he finally realized he needed to tell them everything.

"I'm not sure what we're supposed to do now," stated his dad.

"Me either, but I know I want to use my abilities to help others without becoming the center of attention."

"How in the world are you going to do that?" asked his mother.

"I figure the best use of my powers is to help people during a catastrophe or major disaster. That way I can be helping many people at one time. If I'm not seen a lot, and just help quickly, I can keep my anonymity."

"But what about your education?" asked Mom.

Tyler thought for a moment. "That's a hard one. I can't keep leaving class whenever there is a disaster or something, unless I let someone at school know what I'm up to. But I do want to stay in school and not be home schooled which is my second choice. Besides, I seem to know just about everything. All I have to do is think about it for a split second and bam, there it is."

"How many types of competitive fencing weapons are there?" called out his dad.

"Good one, Dad. There are three, the foil, epee and the saber."

"How many countries are there in the United Nations," asked his mother.

Tyler smiled, "Actually, Mother, next year in my U.S. History class I'll learn that, but since you asked, one hundred ninety-three."

"Okay, wise guy," said Sydney. "What made you the way you are?"

At first Tyler wasn't sure what to say, "That's easy."

"It is?" asked Sydney.

"Mom and Dad," Tyler replied with a loud laugh.

"You know what I mean!" a frustrated Sydney called out.

"And that side of the question I'm still trying to figure out. Haven't received any guidance from my mind on that one, yet."

They spent the rest of the evening trying to figure out how they could help Tyler decide what he should do next. If he really wanted to help people during and after a disaster, then his Dad told him about a good friend of his who worked for the World Disaster Relief Council. Dad said that his friend, Raul Redmond, was one of the first to know about such occurrences. His agency was also one of the first, along with the Red Cross, to assist. He would be an excellent resource for him and someone he knew

Tyler could trust. Their main office was in Westwood, just a few blocks from where they lived.

Tyler thought that meeting with Raul would be a good idea. His dad said he'd call him in the morning and set up an appointment.

As they finished for the evening, Tyler turned to his dad and asked, "Do you know Raul from work, in the financial world?"

"No, actually he goes to our church. You've probably seen him without knowing it."

"We do have a large church, but I don't remember him," Tyler replied.

"Then I guess he's like you want to be, inconspicuous. You'll probably recognize him when you see him."

Chapter Five

A Part-Time Job with the Council

"Are you sure this is what you want to do, Tyler?" his dad asked as they stepped out of their car next to a tall building. "You're going to have to tell him everything."

"You said I could trust him."

"Yes, but this secret is about as big as they come."

"As long as he's not a news reporter it should be all right. Besides, if we find out we can't trust him, what's he going to do, run around LA telling people that he'd met a boy who could fly? I don't think so. I'll just laugh when they ask me."

"Sounds like a good fall back plan if that does happen," said his dad as they both headed into the building.

"Mr. Redmond will see you now," said the receptionist.

"Thanks," replied Tyler.

"Hi, Matt. It's good to see you. This must be your son, Tyler. I believe I've seen him at church. What can I do for you today?"

"Well, Raul, this is something very private and in fact it will seem quite impossible, but we think it could be good for your agency," replied Matt.

"That's an intriguing introduction. You mean good for the World Disaster Relief Council that I direct?"

"Yes," returned Matt. "It may even make you much more effective depending upon how my son Tyler is used."

"You mean Tyler is looking for a job with us?"

"Something like that," Matt replied.

"What exactly did you have in mind?"

"What I'm going to tell you must be kept between us."

"I can assure you, if that's what you want I'll respect your request. I am aware of many things that happen in the world and information involving many people and because of my position that information needs to be kept to myself."

"Thank you," said Matt.

"Now what is this secret and how can your son help us?"

"Mr. Redmond," said Tyler.

"Raul would be fine."

"Then, Raul, I have recently discovered that I have some very special powers that could be of service to you and others and I'm anxious to see how I can use them."

"Are you a computer expert?"

"No, nothing like that, although I can figure out just about anything known to mankind, if that's what you mean."

"That may be useful, but then what else?" Raul asked.

"Let's just say that if Superman existed, I would be him."

Raul sat back in his desk chair slowly. First, he looked long and hard at Tyler then turned to Matt for some assistance.

"I know this isn't a joke, Matt, for I've known you long enough to know that it must be something else."

Matt glanced at Tyler and then looked back at Raul.

"What Tyler told you is absolutely true. He has gained many superhuman powers recently. For what reason, we still don't know. But Tyler's determined to use them for positive things without letting the world know he has them."

Raul pushed forward to get a little closer at Tyler. "What exactly can you do?"

"When I run, I run so fast you wouldn't know I had passed you. I can lift just about anything that can move. Cars and trucks are simple. I have a memory base that seems to include most knowledge known to man. I can hear and see things beyond normal human capabilities. And, I can fly as fast or slow as I desire."

Raul slumped back into his seat.

"This is impossible, Matt. I'm sure nobody set you and Tyler up for this, but it is certainly the most unbelievable thing I've ever heard!"

"Raul," said Tyler, "can that window behind you be opened?"

"Yes, why'd you ask?"

"Would you please open it?"

"I'm not sure why but yes. You do know we're ten stories up?" Raul said as he slid it open.

"Of course, we used the elevator," Tyler replied. "I believe a little demonstration is in order."

"What are you going to do?" Raul asked.

"I'm going to jump out that window and quickly fly to the Santa Monica beach and bring back a handful of wet sand. I will move so fast that I'm sure I won't be noticed."

"Matt, are you going to let him try that?"

"If Tyler says he can do it, he can."

Within a second Tyler had disappeared from the room. He'd focused on several strong reflections to the west.

Raul barely had time to look over at Matt and say, "Are you kidding me!" before Tyler stood in front of him placing a handful of wet sand on his desk.

Raul jumped to his feet and grabbed hold of the sides of his desk as he looked at the sand. He mumbled once or twice shaking his head.

Tyler looked at him and asked, "Would you like some more?"

Raul shook his head "No" as he collapsed back onto his chair.

"That is absolutely the most amazing thing I've ever witnessed! You can fly! Then everything else you told me about your powers is true?" Raul questioned.

"Yes," replied Tyler as he sat back down.

"You could be of service in countless ways! You could help us save many lives! Your powers would be invaluable!" enthused Raul.

"Remember, if I help you, we need to find ways that I can go about my normal life without letting anyone know about my service to the Council," reminded Tyler.

"I can put you on as a part-time hire and call your position 'Special Services.' That way you could come and go into all of our offices and the disaster areas we'd be assisting in."

"That sounds like a good idea, Tyler," said Matt. "I think that might work."

"Now how much do you want to get paid? Set any salary you want," Raul declared.

Tyler hadn't thought about being paid to help others, so he turned to his dad.

"Well, since Tyler's still in high school and living with us he wouldn't need much. Then how about if you simply pay for any expenses he might have? Later, if he's still able to help, and he's living on his own, then he'll need some financial support."

"Anything he wants," replied Raul. "However, we may need to have one or two of my most trustworthy Field Managers in on this. I'm not always available and often don't work on site. They would be the first to know exactly how you could best serve each situation."

"Is that all right with you, Tyler?" asked his dad.

"Yes, except for two things. First, I'd want to meet the managers you'll select before we tell them of my powers to be sure I'm compatible with them. Second, I will only help as long as I'm comfortable with each situation that I'm assigned and I reserve the right to resign at any time."

"Again, yes and yes," said a smiling Raul as he held out his hand.

"There are still a lot of little things we'll need to work out, like how we contact you. Catastrophes and disasters are all different and require a variety of ways to help. Often we have to evaluate what works as we go along."

"I understand that, Raul," replied Tyler.

"Then how should we refer to you? I know you want to remain anonymous."

Tyler looked over at his dad who shrugged his shoulders. "I'm not sure Tyler, what would you like?"

Tyler was thinking when Raul asked, "Just out of curiosity, do you know where your power to do all these things came from?"

Tyler looked at his dad, then at Raul.

"Yes, I do, and since we'll be working closely together, I'll tell you. My powers come from any light source. I seem to absorb it, like a solar cell, and generate an enormous amount of energy. Light, stars, and moonlight all totally energize me. Of course, the sun is my most effective source of power."

"Energy from the sun?" Raul repeated.

"Yes, it seems that way," Tyler replied.

"Then I've got it," replied Raul. "We'll refer to you as Energized Man. That will be our code name for you."

"Energized Man," said his dad. "Not bad."

"I think that will work," replied Tyler as he shook Raul's hand.

At that very moment, Raul's Administrative Assistant, Stacy, came in to his office.

"I'm sorry to interrupt but I must talk to you immediately "

"Raul, that's fine with us. We were just leaving anyway," said Matt as he and Tyler headed towards the door.

"I can't tell you how much we're going to enjoy working with you, Tyler. Thanks for choosing us."

As they stood waiting for the elevator, Matt asked, "Did it go as well as you had hoped?"

"Actually, Dad, even better. There are still a lot of things we need to work out and more that I have to learn. But on the whole, I think I can help them."

Just as the elevator door opened, they heard Raul's voice.

"Just a moment. May I have a word with you?"

"Sure," replied Tyler as they followed him back to his office.

"I was just informed about a problem in the Sudan where we support a hospital. Our sources tell us that a group of local extremists, who don't want us to be there, plan to raid the hospital at any time. We do not have any way of warning them about this. They must evacuate or they all could be captured or harmed. Messages are usually delivered by hand from Khartoum, which often takes several days. Are you willing to try your first assignment and take a message to Elan, my Field Manager?"

"If that's what you need, sure," replied Tyler.

"Then I'll have a message quickly drawn up."

"Are you sure you want to try this, Son?" his dad asked. "You have never been out of the country alone before, much less in a dangerous place like the Sudan."

"I just need to find Elan and then fly back. It shouldn't take me long."

"Okay, Tyler. Here is the message," said Raul as he handed him a sealed envelope.

"I've included the name of the town along with its geographical coordinates. Will this get you there?"

"I seem to have a built in GPS. I just think of the Latitude and Longitude and I'm there."

"Great! How long will it take?"

"I have no idea. Is your window still open?" Tyler asked.

"It is now!" Raul replied as he opened it as far as it would go.

Tyler was out in an instant flying east into the mid-morning sun. He kept repeating the coordinates he'd been given. His flight seemed to automatically adjust, as he focused on various light sources. He could see the earth speeding by below him. He knew he needed to stay between the air routes the local air traffic flew and the higher commercial airlines traveled. At his speed, even though he could see a great distance, he didn't want to have to dodge anything.

Soon Tyler was over the Atlantic Ocean and a few minutes later Africa appeared. He saw mostly desert as he flew down into a desolate village with scattered trees. He landed next to the largest structure in the village. The International Red Cross symbol on the side of the building let him know he'd made the right choice.

He hurried in the door and spotted a young woman dressed in a white gown.

"Excuse me, do you speak English?" he asked.

She appeared very cautious and hesitant to reply. "Yes, a little."

"I have a message for Elan. Is he here?"

"He is in the back. I will get him," she replied as she hurried through a doorway.

Within a moment a man appeared. He also was wearing a white gown. He easily could have been one of the villagers who helped at the hospital, yet he spoke perfect English.

"May I help you? We weren't expecting any communication for another day or two."

"I have an important message from Raul."

"From Raul?" he replied.

"Yes, from Westwood," Tyler answered as he handed Elan the envelope. "It needs to be acted upon immediately."

As Elan read it, he called out, "Quick, everyone, we have to leave right now. We could be raided at any moment! Load our patients into the trucks and alert the villagers!"

Everything came to life. People, whom Tyler hadn't even seen, suddenly appeared.

Elan looked at Tyler and asked, "How did you get here? We only receive communication once or twice a week and never on this day?"

"It's a long story," replied Tyler.

"Since you're here, would you help us load those patients who can't walk onto the trucks?" asked Elan.

Tyler knew he should get back but he did want to help.

"Sure, just point me."

For the next hour Tyler helped load the patients. There were more than he had anticipated. He was very careful not to work beyond his normal ability. One truck full of patients and hospital staff had already left while the second just finished loading.

"Make sure you get on this one, otherwise you'll be left behind," Elan called out.

Just as he nodded to Elan, he noticed a large amount of dust rising from down the road. Soon he identified three trucks speeding towards them, two of which had machine guns mounted on the front.

"Elan! You need to leave now, and fast. Three trucks are rapidly approaching."

"We still have several patients to lift on. There's no way I'm leaving them!"

Tyler knew he had to do something. He was sure the extremists would arrive before Elan had left.

"Leave as soon as you can. Don't worry about me. I'll find a way to avoid them," Tyler yelled and then he was gone.

Within a couple of seconds, he found himself running up behind the third truck. He could see several men with rifles in it. Just as one of the men spotted him Tyler ran alongside and flipped it over. Men and equipment flew around as it rolled several times. He did the same to the other two trucks before they had a chance to fire on him.

Now the extremists could not arrive in time to raid the hospital. In fact, they were probably going to have to walk back to wherever they'd come from.

In the distance Tyler could see the second hospital truck driving away. Even if some of the extremists walked into the village, they'd find most of the people gone.

A second later Tyler flew towards the sun until he'd gained altitude and then turned west. A few minutes later he was back through Raul's window. His dad and Raul had waited in the office.

"Did you get the message to Elan?" Raul asked.

"Yes, just in time. The second hospital truck was getting ready to pull out as the extremists approached."

"But did they all get away safely?" Raul asked.

"I'm sure they did. I was able to get behind the three approaching trucks and flip them over. They're probably going to have to limp back to wherever they came from."

"You flipped them over?" asked his dad.

"Seemed like the right thing to do or Elan and the patients would never have escaped," replied Tyler.

"Then great work...Energized Man," said Raul as he shook his hand. "If you weren't here many people could have been harmed. See, you've already made a big difference to those people."

"Looks like you made the right choice to help Raul and the Council, Tyler," said his father as he patted him on the back.

"Now I think I'd like to go home and grab lunch. Could you drop me off before you head to work, Dad?" Tyler asked.

"I'd be pleased to."

When Tyler arrived home his mother, Kensie, and Sydney wanted to know how the meeting had gone. Tyler told them that he was going to help the Council and in fact had already taken a message to the Sudan for them. After a few more questions Christina fixed him lunch.

After lunch Tyler escaped to his room to look up Sudan on his computer. His mind could answer any questions he had, but he had to ask the right questions. He read about its history and cultural make up along with it's difficult past. He realized that he'd probably saved the lives of many people since the extremists were lethal.

Chapter Six

Bullies and Crisis

The next day Tyler took a bus to Venice Beach to meet Nicholas and Jonathan. His cousins came by bus from Torrance and brought beach supplies, including a football.

They met in front of the shop where they'd bought their swim suits the year before. The shop was located just off of Venice Boulevard on Ocean Front Walk which goes between Santa Monica and Marina Del Rey.

"Hey Tyler, you made it," said Nicholas as Tyler approached.

"You all ready for some football and junk food?" Tyler asked.

"We brought a snack but we've got a mile of junk food places right here," Jonathan replied.

"Let's toss our beach towels down on a good spot near the water, preferably near some cute girls," suggested Tyler.

"By the number of people on the beach today that shouldn't be difficult," added Nicholas.

"Hey, Tyler how's that problem you've got going?" asked Jonathan.

Tyler smiled as he said, "I've found a way to put it to good use. Now I work part time for an international disaster agency. I'm in the Special Service branch and on call if they need me. Yesterday I delivered a message to a Sudanese hospital that saved some lives."

"You mean you just flew over and dropped off a message?" asked Nicholas.

"Well, I helped some when I was there by overturning three trucks filled with armed extremists."

"You what?" said Jonathan.

"What I said. I even have a code name to keep me anonymous."

"What is it? Can you tell us?" asked Nicholas.

"Only you. It's Energized Man, since I get my energy from the sun."

Nicholas smiled and said, "That sure makes sense. It's way better than 'Beam Man'".

"We have a superhero named Energized Man for a cousin," said Jonathan. "Go figure. Are they going to give you a badge or a passport?"

"I don't think so. I probably won't spend enough time in any one location to need a passport. Besides if I'm asked for one, I'll simply fly away. I'm still planning to be just me and go to school and everything."

"It's going to be hard to hide your powers and your new job," stated Nicholas.

The boys picked a spot near a couple of groups of older teenage boys and girls because it was right next to the wet sand where there was better traction for running and throwing.

"Go long," yelled Nicholas as Jonathan took off down the shoreline.

Jonathan made a diving catch and came up with a mouthful of sand.

"Great catch, but it's not time to eat yet," Tyler yelled as Jonathan wiped his mouth and tried to spit out the sand.

"Okay, wise guy, you go long."

Tyler took off concentrating on running a normal speed and Jonathan got off a great pass which Tyler had no problem grabbing.

"I wish I could have thrown it all the way to Santa Monica for you," said Jonathan, "but my arm's just a little short."

"He still would have caught it," replied Nicholas.

"Okay, Nicholas, your turn," said Tyler as Nicholas sped off.

Tyler let him run for a while until he knew it would be a long throw but not an impossibly long throw. When he let go, his arm twitched a bit, sending the football a little further than he expected. Nicholas tried, but couldn't reach it as it bounced down into a group of college kids.

As Nicholas approached them, a large boy, who looked like he played on the line for a football team, stood up.

"Sorry about that errant throw. We'll try going the other direction with that football next time," said Nicholas with a smile as he held out his hands for the ball.

"What ball?" replied the boy holding the football as he stood up.

"The one you're holding," replied Nicholas reaching for the ball.

"You know you bounced the ball off my girlfriend's back," he said.

Nicholas looked down at his girlfriend who had just turned around to look at him and said, "I'm sorry we hit you. It was an accident."

"You're forgiven," she replied with a laugh and a smile.

"No, you're not. I saw your friend throw it deliberately at us."

"I'm sure he had no intention of doing that. Why would he?" asked Nicholas.

"Maybe for some attention from my girlfriend," the large teen returned, "which isn't going to happen."

"If I could please have our ball, I'll leave you alone," said Nicholas as he reached for the ball.

The boy instantly knocked Nicholas down and threw the football hard against his back. Another boy stood up, picked up the football, and also threw it down at Nicholas saying, "My turn! Oh, I'm sorry, kid, I didn't mean to do that!"

Then the two of them laughed.

Tyler finally noticed what was happening up the beach and instantly appeared.

"I'm pretty sure my cousin apologized for my bad throw as I do. There is no cause to be bullies'" he said.

"Looks like you belong in the sand too!" the boy said as he gave Tyler a hard push.

Tyler just stood still and didn't move an inch. Actually, the boy who had pushed him bounced back shaking his wrists.

"Hey, what's going on here?" he said.

"Nothing," replied Tyler. "If you'll just give us our ball back, we'll leave."

Now two other boys stood up.

"Hey maybe you'd better lay down in the sand before we make you," said one of them.

"Just give me the ball and we'll leave," replied Tyler again as Nicholas stood next to him and Jonathan came up the beach.

At that point the first boy dove at Tyler as if to pick him up.

Tyler quickly stepped aside as the attacker fell face first onto the sand.

"It's awfully nice of you to show us how we're supposed to lay on the sand," Tyler couldn't help but say.

The group began to laugh at their friend, but the girls appeared to be unhappy about the way their friends were treating the younger boys.

"You need to respect your elders, boy," threatened the tall blond kid standing to Tyler's right as he charged towards him.

Instantly Tyler knelt down as the blond boy attacked. This caused the boy to fall right over him. Then Tyler quickly stood up and threw him about twenty feet into the sand behind him.

The third boy ran at Tyler who just stood his ground. As the boy hit against him unsuccessfully, Tyler used both his arms to firmly push him back until he lay on his back about fifteen feet away.

"Wow, another demonstration of what you want us to do. Thank You. Now may I please have the football?" Tyler asked.

Every eye was on Tyler.

Someone said, "How'd he do that?"

The first boy's girlfriend crawled over and picked up the ball from the sand near her boyfriend.

She tossed it to Tyler saying, "I'm sorry about the way our friends acted, but I'm sure they won't be bothering you again."

All of her friends nodded and laughed in agreement.

As Tyler, Nicholas, and Jonathan walked back to their beach towels, they could see the boys slowly getting up.

"Man, Tyler, you sure showed them," said Jonathan.

"I didn't want to do that but I did get a bit upset when they were making fun of us. Anyway, I tried not to hurt them or show them too much of my strength," replied Tyler.

"They'll be trying to figure that out for a long time." said Nicholas.

"Okay, now who's going long?" asked Tyler spinning the football in his right hand.

"I am!" stated Jonathan. "Although I think I'd better run the opposite direction this time."

As Jonathan took off the loud sound of an approaching helicopter vibrated through the air.

Tyler's throw almost hit Jonathan who was having trouble seeing because the sand was blowing into his eyes. The helicopter landed about a hundred feet from where he had stopped. Tyler noticed that Jonathan was trying to cover both his eyes and ears at the same time.

The sound of a helicopter vibrated through the air.

"What in the world is that copter pilot trying to do?" yelled Nicholas. "If he's trying to annoy everyone on the beach then he's succeeded."

"This is really strange," replied Tyler.

A man jumped out of the helicopter and headed towards Tyler and Nicholas.

"Okay, did we mistakenly hit someone with the football again?" asked Nicholas as the man approached.

The man was wearing a suit and seemed to be in a great hurry.

"Which of you is Energized Man?" he yelled out to the boys.

"Who wants to know?" replied Tyler as the man stopped next to them.

"If it helps, then I'm Seth, a colleague of Raul."

Tyler looked him over for a second before replying, "In that case, I am. How'd you find me?"

"That's what we do when there is a problem," he replied.

"Then you need my help?" asked Tyler who was already pretty sure when he spotted the helicopter starting to land on the busy beach that he was the reason.

"Yes, you'll need to come with me so I can explain," Seth replied.

"Then I'd like to have my cousins come also."

The man stepped closer to Tyler.

"This is very important and not a sight-seeing expedition. Besides are they aware **of your** relationship with Raul and the reason why we need you?" he asked.

"Yes, and they can be trusted. I just wanted them to see how things are going to work for me."

"This is very irregular. If you insist they come, then bring them along."

Tyler yelled at his cousins to gather their stuff and follow him to the helicopter.

A small crowd of people, including the college kids had gathered nearby.

Tyler could hear one of the boys saying, "I told you there was something up with that kid."

As the helicopter began to lift off from the beach, Tyler asked, "What's happening?"

Seth turned to him and said, "A few minutes ago we received word that a sightseeing boat had just lost power north of Malibu and had somehow washed up against the rocky shore. The surf is pounding against it and no one is able to get off because of the rocks and the hundred-foot cliff above them. Even the emergency rescue teams are having trouble getting safely down to them and they're much too close to shore for a sea rescue."

"Has anyone been injured?" Tyler asked.

"Not yet, but the boat is almost on its side and starting to break up. According to the sightseeing company's records there are twelve people on board and they're barely hanging on.

"Raul figures that the odds aren't in their favor and it's a disaster in the making. That's why he took a chance in getting you involved even though you wanted to remain anonymous."

"Then get me as close as you can so I can check it out."

Tyler studied the situation.

The pilot had already headed north towards Malibu, so Tyler was able to see that the sea was much rougher and the wind much stronger than where they had been on the beach.

"Circle around about a thousand feet above the boat," ordered Tyler as they approached.

Tyler studied the situation for a moment trying to figure out the best way to save the passengers without being identified. He wondered how long he could hold his breath under water. The answer came to him immediately.

"Keep circling and keep the door area clear!" he said as he suddenly jumped out of the helicopter.

Nicholas and Jonathan watched Tyler drop a few feet and then disappear.

Tyler quickly focused on a bright reflection near the boat and headed down. He hit the water about a hundred feet from the boat then rapidly swam under water towards it. He saw that the boat's hull was still in one piece and that it had taken on some water from its angle and the surf.

First, from under the water, Tyler stabilized the boat by gently pushing it from the rocks and into deeper water. He made sure that it was floating properly as he pushed on the disabled prop and moved it along the shore to a small beach cove formed in the side of the cliff. He forced the boat far enough up through the surf and onto the sand until it was safely held on shore until the rescue crews could make their way down.

Within a few minutes Tyler appeared through the helicopter door.

"Wow!" gasped Nicholas. "That was amazing! You really can do just about anything."

"For a moment I thought you were a goner when you stayed under the water so long," added Jonathan.

Seth just sat shaking his head and said, "Now I understand why Raul sent me to get a kid to help. You were amazing! I can see why he feels so strongly about your ability to help the council...and the world."

"I just try to help where I can," Tyler added. "I hope no one was able to get a good look at me."

"I doubt that," said Seth. "You were under water most of the time."

As they flew towards Torrance, Nicholas and Jonathan kept patting Tyler on the back. They seemed exhilarated to have seen what their cousin was capable of.

"If there is ever anything we can do to help," said Jonathan, "let us know!"

Nicholas stared at Jonathan and asked, "And how fast can you fly?"

"Well, you know what I mean," Jonathan replied.

The pilot spotted the large grounds of an elementary school near Nicholas and Jonathan's home and quickly landed.

"Hey, thanks for the ride," said Nicholas.

"Yeah, I've never been brought home in a chopper before," added Jonathan.

"See ya!" Tyler said with a wave as the helicopter headed towards Westwood.

"Do you mind if we land on the top of Raul's office building?" Seth asked. "I believe he'd like a word with you."

"Sure, but I will need to get home soon."

"I'll be glad to send you home in a cab from there...unless, of course, you'd rather, uh, fly."

"Home's not that far, but a cab would be great," replied Tyler.

Raul was waiting in his office.

"Welcome back!" he shouted as he shook Tyler's hand. "You never cease to amaze me! Take a look at this. I recorded the news coverage of the sight-seeing boat emergency."

Tyler watched as the commentators discussed the disaster that was about to happen. No one could figure out how the passengers could be saved given the circumstances. The cameras suddenly rose to see a distant helicopter hovering high above the boat. They commented on whether it was going to try to get close enough to attempt a dangerous cable rescue.

"Look!" yelled one of the newsmen. "The boat is upright and moving away from the rocks! Is the engine working now? How did it push off away from the rocks?"

"I have no idea," replied another newsman. "But it's moving north towards that small sandy cove."

"This is a miracle or something. Look, the passengers are okay and climbing down onto the beach!" yelled the first newsman. "Absolutely amazing!"

"And that's what I wanted you to see. I hope you see how much good you can do. You saved them and no one but us knows how it happened. Tyler, you are amazing!"

Tyler felt proud of himself and honored that Raul would take the time to praise and thank him.

"I really appreciate your praise and support, Raul," replied Tyler. "But I'm still just learning what I can do and how I can help. I've got a long way to go before I can figure all this out."

When Tyler arrived home, he was greeted by Kensie, Sydney, and his parents. They had been watching the news about the pending disaster and had figured out that Tyler was in some way involved.

"So, how'd you do that?" asked Kensie.

"Oh, so now whenever something extraordinary happens you figure I've got to be involved," replied Tyler.

"Well?" asked Christina.

"They picked us up by helicopter on the beach and took us to the boat."

"Us?" asked Matt.

"Yeah, I asked them to take Nicholas and Jonathan with us so they could see the kind of work I'm doing for the Council. I told them my cousins knew everything anyway."

"Are they all right?" asked Christina.

"We flew them home and landed on the old school field near their house. They seemed to enjoy it."

"Okay, I guess. I hope Nathan and Cathy don't mind them doing all that," mentioned Matt.

"Anyway, we hovered high above the boat as I figured out the best way to save them without being recognized. So, I found out that I can also hold my breath and swim very fast under water. I freed the boat and pushed it to a nearby sandy cove. That's it! Oh, Raul wanted to thank me so we landed on his building and I came home in a cab."

"Then we were right. It was you, again," said Sydney.

"I hope this doesn't happen too often," said Matt. "You still have your own life to live and school to finish."

"And all this sounds mega dangerous to me," cautioned Christina.

"Since I seem to be indestructible, Mom, I don't feel that it's too dangerous for me."

"Kryptonite!" said Kensie.

"What do you mean by that?" asked Christina.

"Well, it seems to me that every superhero has a weakness. Superman's was Kryptonite. Maybe Tyler has one too," she replied.

Tyler laughed.

"Then I sure hope it's not chocolate or pizza. I'd hate to stay away from those!"

"All levity aside," said Matt, "you really do need to check to see if you have any weaknesses as soon as possible."

"I'll do that Dad. But so far all I keep discovering are more strengths!"

Chapter Seven

Wake and More Work

That early evening after dinner, Tyler decided to take a run around the golf course. He told his parents that he needed to unwind. He knew in the cool evening, without much light to overly stimulate him, he could just take it easy and run.

Tyler headed west on Pico then down Patricia Avenue and cut east until he'd just about circled the Rancho Park and Hillcrest Golf courses. As he hit Pico again heading east, he felt that he was not alone. When he was passing through Pico and Motor Avenue, a large white van cut in front of him. As he slowed down a black limousine shot out from the Fox Studio parking area and boxed him in.

Two men had gotten out of the van and were approaching him.

Tyler was startled, but knew he could take care of any problem that might present itself. So, he stopped to see what they wanted.

"I'm not sure what you want, but it would be to your benefit to be very careful about what you're going to do," Tyler stated.

The two men stopped a few feet away.

"Our employer in the limo would like to have a word with you. That's all," the taller man said.

"Then this is a poor way of asking for a simple conversation."

"Our employer is rather secretive and likes to do the unexpected," the man continued.

"Then tell him if he pulls the limo over to the curb, I'll talk to him," Tyler replied.

Immediately the limo pulled over just in front of Tyler as the van circled around and moved in behind it. Tyler walked over to the back-door window which had just been rolled down.

A middle-aged man with slightly graying hair looked out the window.

"Sorry to surprise you like this, Tyler, but I needed to get your attention when there weren't others around," he said.

"Well, now you have it," returned Tyler. "So what do you want?"

"Why does everyone always feel I want something?" he replied.

"Probably because you pick a dark and out of the way spot to introduce yourself."

"Then I apologize. My name is Wake and I'm here to talk business."

"How do you know my name?" Tyler asked.

"If you don't mind sitting inside the limo for a moment, I'll let you know."

Realizing that he could handle just about anything Tyler decided to move into the Limo.

"Doing something illegal to me would be very bad for you and your men," Tyler warned.

"I'm very much aware of the things you can do. That's what I want to talk to you about."

Tyler was surprised but tried not to show it.

"Okay, what do you want to talk about?"

"Mostly you."

"Why?" Tyler asked.

"Let's just say you could be of great assistance to me."

"I don't understand," relied Tyler.

"I know all about you. I first found out about you when you freed the two passengers from a burning car and then caught a rolling ambulance on West Olympic and Century."

Now Wake had Tyler's complete attention. Someone had identified him, but how? And if he knew Tyler was the one who had done these things who else might know?

"And today, when you saved the sightseeing boat, I must say, I was quite impressed," Wake stated with a smile.

Now Tyler was worried. What did this man want? He could blow Tyler's cover and undo everything he had done trying to remain anonymous.

"What makes you think I had anything to do with those things?" he asked.

"Nothing happens in the Los Angeles area without me knowing. My influence and contacts are quite remarkable."

"Then what if it was me? How does that have anything to do with you?" Tyler asked.

"Again, I'll say that anything that happens in Los Angeles actually does affect me. I try to keep control of what takes place. I'm kind of like a caretaker for the city."

"I know you're not the Mayor or the Chief of Police, so why do I interest you?"

"Because we may be able to assist each other."

"How?" Tyler asked.

"As I said, I have many interests in this city, and sometimes I need some specialized help. With your unique skills you could fill that role."

"You mean you're offering me some kind of a job?"

"Not as you'd know it. Besides, you already have job with the World Disaster Relief Council."

Tyler was surprised to see how impressive Wake's information was.

"You are aware of many things. My identity, as you apparently know, is important for me to keep a secret so I can be more effective in helping."

"And I'd like to keep it that way also." said Wake. "All I ask is that once in a while you help me solve a problem that I feel only you could successfully complete, like sort of my 'man on call'."

"You know that I plan to go to school and be available at a moment's notice to assist the Council. Now how would I have time to help you? And even if I could, what kinds of things would you use me for? In no way am I going to do anything unlawful," Tyler added.

Wake made a wheezing soft laugh.

"I promise, I won't ask you to do anything that is illegal, just once in a while something that's 'unique'."

"And why should I consent to this?"

"For one, we could be of help to each other. I know about potentially harmful events even before Raul. Also, I may be the only person, besides your family and of course Raul, who knows who you are, and I plan to keep it that way if you assist me once in a while."

"So your offer comes with a subtle threat?" Tyler asked.

"Let's just say that my reach is far, and sooner or later I get what I want. However, I'd rather keep this on a 'you help me and I'll help you' basis. There are a lot of doors I can open for you in many areas."

Tyler wasn't sure what to make of Wake. He obviously was someone to take seriously, someone who did have him in a head lock. Tyler needed time to think.

"Let me think about this. I understand the importance you place upon this kind of relationship. Give me a couple of days and I'll let you know. Do you have a card with a phone number?"

"Don't worry, just like tonight, I'll find you. Have a good evening," Wake replied, as Tyler stepped from his limousine.

As Wake's entourage pulled away, Tyler took note of the makes, models, and license numbers of their cars.

While he ran the last few blocks home, he couldn't help but smile. Kensie may be right. Was Wake possibly his kryptonite?

When Tyler arrived back home, he decided he'd tell his dad about Wake and his strange request. Matt listened quietly as Tyler reviewed the conversation.

"It sounds to me like you've met up with a powerful manipulator who feels that he controls Los Angeles. It is interesting that he knows all about you and your deal with Raul. I don't like the sound of it.

It does look like he's trying to threaten you to do something he wants in the future. I believe a visit with Raul is in order. If Wake knows all about you, then Raul probably knows who this man is. I'll call first thing in the morning. I wouldn't worry too much about Mr. Wake. If he truly knows your powers, then I'm sure he will be very cautious in regards to you and your family. If necessary, you could really bother him if he became a threat."

Tyler's dad made the appointment the next morning so he and Tyler could meet with Raul on the way to work.

"Good morning! It's a pleasure to see both of you so soon. Have a seat. Matt, you said that this had to do with a man named Wake?"

"Yes, it does. I'll let Tyler fill you in."

Raul sat perfectly still throughout Tyler's account of his meeting with Wake.

"So, this is an important twist. I do know Wake and he is a very powerful man who moves in the shadows within Los Angeles. He seems to have eyes and ears everywhere and he is not to be taken lightly. His actual name is Walter Pressen. His associates call him Wake, because he plows ahead like a ship in water. But others say they call him that because in business he occasionally leaves behind an associate's funeral."

"I understand," replied Tyler, "but how could he know about me, much less about us?"

Raul thought for a moment before answering.

"He could have figured it out if he'd had his associates talk to the people who had been at the scene of your saves. Perhaps some money exchanged hands to buy cell phone photos that the police never saw. In regard to us working together, only someone who knew you came to me and either speculated about it or heard of our arrangement, could have known. I may have an employee who isn't following our Confidentiality Agreement."

"Then I think we need to work together in utmost secrecy and find out exactly who and what Wake does. I think we should start with the license numbers of the two vehicles that stopped me," Tyler said as he handed a piece of paper to Raul."

"Great!" replied Raul. "I'll ask Stacy to run these through our friends at the DMV."

"But what should we...I mean Tyler do about Wake's offer?" asked Matt.

"I believe that since we know little about Wake's activities at this time, it would be wise to make the same arrangement with him as you have with me. At least until we have more information."

"And what would that be again?" asked Matt

"That Tyler will help only occasionally and only as long as he's comfortable with the situation. Also, he should reserve the right to turn down an assignment and to resign when he feels the relationship with Wake is no longer positive and helpful"

"That makes sense to me," said Tyler.

"I guess that's the best we can do for now," agreed Matt.

Just then Stacy returned with the information about the two vehicles Wake had used.

"What did you find out?" asked Raul.

"They are both registered to a consulting company named Great Minds International. Its employees analyze and evaluate management decisions in order to help companies improve their business practices and their effectiveness. It seems to be a real brain trust company with many business clients," replied Stacy.

"I'm familiar with them," said Raul.

"And I've heard of them too. They are supposed to be very good at what they do," added Matt.

"Then it seems to me," replied Tyler, "that Wake could be asking for favors that are legitimate and not something I'll have to worry about."

"It looks that way, but things aren't always as they seem. You still need to be careful," suggested Raul.

Stacy reappeared at the door.

"Yes, Stacy," said Raul.

"That coal mine cave-in near Billings, Wyoming, that you asked me to keep an eye on, has gotten worse."

Raul stood up and asked, "In what way?"

"The rescue teams are having trouble breaking through to the forty-eight miners trapped below. It looks like they may run out of air because the air supply system is apparently damaged. One possible rescue tunnel is partly flooded, and another they've been working on seems to be blocked by debris from the cave-in," reported Stacy.

"How much time do they have?"

"The rescue team manager guessed maybe ten hours," she replied.

"Hopefully they can at least open up an airway before it runs out," replied Raul.

"Is there something I can do?" asked Tyler.

"I'm not sure. The cave-in happened several hours ago. The rescue crews were hoping to use the tunnel that's flooded and now, like Stacy said, they are working down a tunnel that's blocked. It's a very dangerous situation. In most disaster situations we would have already sent a team to determine the kind of help they need, but in cases like this we have to let the experts do their jobs before we know how we can help."

Tyler turned to his dad then back to Raul. "Are you sure I couldn't be of some help?"

"I wasn't going to bother you since it looked like they had it under control...but now I'm not sure how we can help."

"Raul," said Matt, "is there any way you could talk to the mining company's Chief Engineer to determine what possible alternative plans they have?"

"In situations like these they have to match their plans with the personnel and equipment they have."

"Yeah, but they don't have an Energized Man, do they?" Matt asked.

"You know, I could find out if there are other ways to approach the situation if they had the right personnel or equipment. Maybe there would be a way for Tyler to help," replied Raul as he quickly picked up the phone.

After several minutes Stacy brought a small pile of papers that the mining company had faxed to them.

"Great! Here are the schematics of the tunnels and location of the cave-in!" exclaimed Raul.

"Looks like they've marked the two tunnels they hoped to use," said Matt as he eyed the tunnel map.

"And there is where the water is blocking the first tunnel," added Tyler as he pointed to the markings on the map.

"Yeah, it looks like the water built up in the tunnel right here and can't drain out," noted Raul.

"It's right next to the tunnel where the miners are trapped," said Tyler.

"Yes, that's where they were first hoping to go," said Raul. "It's just a few feet between the two, but with the flooding, no way."

"Then what's keeping the water in that section of the tunnel?" asked Matt.

"It looks to me like there could be a partial cave-in further down in that tunnel that caused the water to back up," answered Raul.

"And what's this just below where the two tunnels almost come together?" asked Matt.

"I'm not sure. Let me make a quick call to the Chief Engineer," replied Raul as he picked up the phone.

After a brief conversation Raul marked several points on the map and then hung up.

"He says that marks an airway to a lower tunnel."

"Then why isn't the water draining through that into the lower tunnel?" questioned Tyler.

"Because there is a small water tight vent that can only be opened from the flooded tunnel. If that were opened the water would probably drain out to that point allowing the workmen to cut through to where the trapped miners are located."

"Couldn't they use a scuba diver to swim down and open it?" asked Matt.

"They considered that idea, but felt it was very dangerous. There is too much water and if the vent could be opened the diver would be at risk as the draining water pulled him towards the vent."

"I know I can stay under water for a long time," said Tyler.

"Okay, but it's also pitch-black down there and another cave-in could happen once the water drains and the tunnels walls are weakened," replied Raul.

"Raul," said Tyler, "can you get your hands on a water tight head lamp? I can see rather well in the dark, but that would make it a sure thing."

"Then you're willing to risk the tunnel and the water?" asked Raul.

"Yes, but only as a last resort. Did they say how long it would take to break through the tunnel wall if they drained the water?" Tyler asked.

"The Chief Engineer did mention that they only needed about two hours to break through."

"Then I'll wait and see if they are able to solve the problem in the next few hours. If not then I'll leave in plenty of time for them to break through. That is if I can get down the tunnel, through the water, find the vent, and am able to open it," said Tyler.

"If it looks too dangerous then don't do it," said Matt.

"I'll have to see, Dad, and then decide. The lives of forty-eight men depend on me succeeding."

"Okay," said Raul, "I'll give you a call if they need you. In the meantime, I'll send a head lamp to you."

At home Tyler studied the map so he knew the location of the mine in Wyoming.

He also became more familiar with the mine, how it worked, and its many tunnels. After several hours he received a call from Raul. The lamp had arrived just before the call. Within a moment Tyler took off from his porch heading northeast.

Again, he flew in the airway between the commercial and private airspace. Since he was heading northeast in the late afternoon, he couldn't focus on the sun that was now behind him. He constantly needed to look for light sources from reflections to the rising moon.

Following the latitude and longitude locations he had memorized, he soon arrived at the mine. He circled the area, getting his bearings before he dove to the proper tunnel entrance. Since the tunnel was flooded and the rescue crew's attention was drawn to another tunnel, no one was around to see him land and run in.

Tyler turned on his head lamp, and paused to evaluate the situation. Then he ran down several hundred feet and arrived at the water.

From the map it looked like the water had built up about a hundred feet above the air vent that he needed to find. Tyler dove in and began swimming down. The head lamp helped a lot since it was as dark as it could possibly be. Soon he found a small hatch door similar to one that might be found on a submarine. Its lever handle protruded to the side. Tyler took hold and was able to pull it up and open.

The water started rushing down the air vent to the lower tunnel. He felt the powerful suction pull him towards the vent. He pushed off the tunnel wall and tried swimming as hard as he could to get away from its pull. Instead he found himself against the vent blocking the water from going through. He still had plenty of air but he was being held hostage against the vent. He tried again to get away by grabbing the rough surface of the tunnel. If he could only move away from the vent and let the water all flow out, he could simply run up the tunnel.

Finally, he was able to climb above the vent where there was less pull and where he could hold his position as the water streamed through. When the only water left in the tunnel was below the air vent, Tyler quickly ran up to the tunnel's opening.

No one was around to learn that the water had been cleared. He hadn't thought about that. How could he tell them without giving himself away?

As he looked across the grounds, he noticed a woman with a young boy talking to a man who was dressed like a miner. Tyler worked his way towards them trying to keep out of sight. Fortunately, the young boy wasn't very interested in the conversation and kept looking around. When the boy looked his direction, Tyler stepped out from behind the large barrel he'd been behind. Taking off his head lamp and holding it out to the boy, Tyler took a couple of steps forward. Understanding the gesture, the boy smiled and walked towards him.

"Hi!" Tyler said.

The boy smiled and said, "Hi."

"I'll give you this head lamp if you take a message to that man who is talking to your mother."

The boy turned towards his mother, then looked back at Tyler.

"Okay," he replied.

"Tell the miner that someone told you that the tunnel was now clear of water and they can save the men by cutting through, all right?"

The boy smiled and nodded as Tyler handed him the lamp. While the boy ran back to the woman, Tyler jumped into the sky and headed towards the setting sun.

In the short time it took Tyler to fly back to Westwood and land on top of Raul's office building, Raul had received a call from Billings saying that somehow the water had drained. As Tyler came in Raul gave him a big hug and told him that it looked like he saved the forty-eight miners. The rescue crews were already in the water-free tunnel and cutting through to bring them out.

Tyler was pleased and realized how important his new powers were. He figured that if he could do any job in the world, helping others with these new found powers would be at the top of his list. He realized that he still had a lot to learn, both about his powers and how he'd use them in the future.

By the time his cab arrived home, Tyler's parents and sisters were there to greet him. They'd been watching the CNN report on the tunnel rescue. The rescue crew was almost through and had heard tapping from the other side of their dig.

His family, of course had all kinds of questions for him. How long did it take him to get to Wyoming? How difficult was it to drain the tunnel? How much water did he have to swim through? Did anybody see him? Tyler patiently answered all their questions. He knew that they wanted to support him and be a small part of his adventures. Besides, he kind of enjoyed the attention.

Chapter Eight

The Window Man and Brace

That night Tyler woke up again before dawn as self-doubt crept in.

"What am I doing?" he thought. *"This is very dangerous stuff. I've been lucky so far. I was almost trapped by the water pressure today. Why me? And where did these powers come from all of a sudden? What am I supposed to do about Wake? If he tries to force me to do something I don't want to do, will he hurt my family? And if he tries, do I fight back and destroy his network of associates? The last thing I want to do is hurt others unless it's absolutely the only way."*

Tyler realized he had a lot of questions that needed an answer. He was worried because even his many abilities couldn't tell him his future.

The following morning a groggy Tyler woke up and remembered that he had told Kensie he would walk with her to the Century Center Plaza. Kensie had said she needed another outfit and a few more accessories for her high school début.

"You sure look tired," stated Kensie as they walked up Olympic. "Did you have another one of those nights?"

"No, if you mean did I go flying or something. I just had my usual lying awake worrying thing again."

"You need to get used to your talents and just enjoy helping others. If these talents disappear as fast as you discover them, you're still my brother and a smart guy. Besides, I'm sure you could easily be successful as a barber."

"Thanks, but I kind of had my mind set on being a jet pilot."

"So, what's the difference? As it is, you can fly without a plane and if you lose that power you can fly in one. Either way it looks like some kind of flying is in your future!"

"Tell me again. Why do you need more clothes?" Tyler asked.

"Because girls can't simply wear the same two different shirts and pair of pants to school each day like a boy can. We have to, you know, mix it up a bit, be fashionable, so we'll be noticed."

"It seems to me that it has to do with your own self-image. It simply makes you feel better," replied Tyler.

"That's pretty much it," replied Kensie.

Soon they were walking through a courtyard surrounded by stores of all types.

Kensie paused in front of one of her favorite dress shops.

"I think I'll start here. Why don't we meet at BJ's Restaurant in about an hour and have some lunch?"

"That's fine with me. I'll be at the Apple store. There are a couple of things I need to ask about and I may stop at my favorite yogurt shop on the way."

"Snack all you want. As for me I'll need to be more careful so I can fit into the dress I plan on buying. See you at BJ's."

Tyler waved and headed toward his favorite yogurt shop. When he thought he heard someone screaming, he stopped and looked around but no one else seemed to hear it. Looking above the shorter buildings around him and toward the south-east, his heightened vision locked onto a strange sight. When he squinted to take a closer look, he saw a man hanging by a rope about five stories down the side of the twenty-five story Constellation Building. Apparently, he was a window washer. One of the cables that held up his work platform had broken and now he was swaying in the wind.

Tyler looked to the top of the building to see if anyone was coming to his aid. Seeing no one, Tyler knew what he needed to do.

"*Darn it!*" he thought.

He couldn't believe that in the last few days all these crisis situations had taken place when he was around. He'd never experienced even one before, not that he could have helped anyway, but he could have watched while those trained to help did their jobs.

"*Fine, now how do I do this without anyone knowing?*"

Tyler noticed that Macy's Department store was next to him. It had a third story roof. If he could find the stairs and get onto the roof, he could fly up without anyone seeing him take off. As he thought about this, he moved quickly through the store, found the stairs, and headed up.

Just as he figured, the door to the roof was locked. Since he had no time to find another way in, he put his shoulder to it and broke off the lock. From the roof he located the sun right over the top of the Constellation Building and jumped towards it. In a moment he was on the roof looking down at the window washer who was still screaming for help.

Tyler saw that the platform was hooked from the roof and the ratchet that moved it up and down was located on the platform below. It couldn't be used by the washer since it required both left and right cables to be intact. So, he grabbed the left cable and started pulling up the washer and the platform which must have weighed at least four hundred pounds.

The screaming stopped as the man holding on for his life realized he was moving up and that someone had come to his rescue.

Tyler pulled the man up to within a foot or two of the roof. He quickly tied off the cable on some nearby pipes. When the man reached up to pull himself safely onto the building, Tyler quickly jumped back to the Macy's roof and walked down the stairs into the promenade area. He looked up at the top of the Constellation Building and now saw two people with the window washer.

Tyler smiled when he realized that once again, he was able to help someone and remain anonymous. He decided to reward himself with some of his favorite yogurt ice cream.

As he made his way past the Tesla car store, a tall man in a dark suit stepped in front of him, forcing Tyler to stop.

"Very nice work," the man said with a smile.

Tyler wasn't sure what to say or what this man wanted so he just nodded and smiled.

"Yes, Mr. Wake is impressed again."

"How do you always know what I'm doing?" Tyler asked before he could stop himself.

"You know the answer, Tyler. We know everything, but that's not what I'm here for. Mr. Wake wants to know the answer to his request."

Wisely Tyler decided to tell him what he, Raul, and his dad had agreed to.

"Tell him that I will occasionally help him as long as I'm comfortable with the situation. Also, I reserve the right to refuse to take an assignment. I also can resign if I feel the relationship with him is no longer positive."

The tall man stood there for a moment with a slight smile on his face.

"I will pass on your response and we'll get back to you shortly," the man said as he turned and walked back into the store.

Tyler continued to the yogurt shop. He couldn't believe that in spite of all his powers and indestructibility someone like Wake's associate could make him feel so vulnerable, actually a little scared. He was very aware that he was new to this superhero stuff and needed more confidence. Mostly he was bothered by the fact that he didn't know how Wake would respond to his answer. Wake could make things very difficult for him if he wanted to.

However, waiting inside the yogurt shop for him was his favorite yogurt combination. He grabbed a medium size cup and checked out the seven flavors of the day. Sure enough they had the dark chocolate and the tart vanilla. Now after a scoop of the small chocolate chips and one of ground peanuts, he topped it off with some small marshmallows. He usually added quite a few of the marshmallows. Since they priced the yogurt by weight, a bunch of light marshmallows would add hardly anything to the price.

When he headed out the door enjoying his first few spoonfuls, he heard a voice behind him.

"Well, what do you think?"

As he pulled the spoon from his mouth, he noticed Kensie standing behind him posing in a new dress.

"Wow!" Tyler belted out as he then realized he was being a little too loud.

"So, that's good?" Kensie replied.

Tyler decided he needed to choose his words carefully.

"Actually, you look great. You look like a high school upper classman and not a newbie. If you are trying to gain confidence and want to be noticed, you picked the right outfit. I also like the scarf," he added trying to be sure he noted the accessory she'd also purchased.

"Then I'll keep it!" she said as she took Tyler's spoon and scooped out a large bite.

"Hey, if you want some, I'll buy you your own."

"Actually," Kensie said, "since you offered, I would like my own yogurt."

"Besides," Tyler added as he paid for his sister's yogurt, "the one I'm eating is my treat for saving a window washer from a fall off the Constellation Building a few minutes ago."

"You did what?"

As Tyler was explaining what happened to the window washer, the tall man in the dark suit reappeared and pulled up a chair to sit down next to them. Tyler was surprised to see the man so soon and concerned that he appeared when he was with someone else, especially Kensie.

"Sorry to have to bother you like this, Tyler, but it's rather important. By the way, my name is Brace," he said as he held out his hand.

Tyler put his cup of yogurt down and shook it. Trying to be polite Tyler introduced Kensie.

"And this is my sister, Kensie."

The man again reached out his hand and Kensie, who seemed quite surprised by the interruption, shook it.

"Yes, Kensie, I know who you are and it's nice to meet you," he replied.

"I'm also aware that you are familiar with your brother's, let's say, 'situation.' So, since my business with your brother is urgent, I apologize for having to bother you."

"If it's that important then you're apology's accepted. Would you like me to leave you two alone?" asked Kensie.

"That's up to Tyler," replied Brace.

"If that's the case then you're welcome to stay, Kensie."

"Then I will," she replied as she picked up her yogurt again.

Tyler looked at Brace and asked, "Then what is this urgent news?"

"First," said Brace, "Mr. Wake will accept your conditions for your business relationship."

Tyler glanced at Kensie then replied, "Agreed."

"Fine," said Brace with a slight smile. "Then second, for the more urgent part, Mr. Wake has an immediate assignment for you."

Tyler swallowed hard and replied, "That was quick."

"Well, Mr. Wake does not like to wait when a problem arises."

"Then how can I be of service?" asked Tyler.

"This is a little problem that needs immediate attention that only your skill set can solve. Otherwise he would never have bothered you at this time."

"Okay, then what is it?"

"First, how high have you flown?"

Tyler was surprised by the question. "I really haven't given it much thought, but probably up to where the oxygen disappears."

"Do you think you'd have any trouble going higher than that?"

"How much higher?" Tyler asked curiously.

"About one hundred and thirty miles," Brace replied as Kensie dropped her cup on the table.

"Why that's up with the satellites!" she exclaimed.

"Precisely," replied Brace.

At this point, Tyler put his cup down and stuck his spoon deep into the remaining yogurt.

"Then what you're saying is that Mr. Wake needs some help with a satellite?"

"Yes, and it needs to be accomplished right away."

"I'm not so sure about this. Why is it so important?" Tyler asked.

"One of the many businesses that Mr. Wake is involved with is shipping. You are aware that the Los Angeles and San Pedro harbors are major shipping ports?"

"Yes, I've been to them before."

"Then you may know that most shipping navigation is guided by Navstats Satellites. The problem is that one of the major satellites that guides these ships is about to come down. Its orbit is now too low. Mr. Wake would like you to go up and push it slightly higher and also increase its speed."

Tyler slumped back in his chair and Kensie seemed to be at a loss for words.

Finally, Tyler said, "Great first assignment! I'm sure glad he didn't pick something simple in order to test our relationship."

"That's just the problem, he has no choice. This would put many ships in a very dangerous situation. There is no other way to solve the problem except to let a very valuable and expensive satellite burn up as it falls to earth."

"That I can understand, but I don't know if I have the ability to solve the problem," replied Tyler.

"We know you've no experience with situations like this, but Mr. Wake has every confidence in your ability to succeed. Please give it some thought. We only have three days. Here is a sheet that explains what needs to be done and the speed and positioning of the satellite at any particular time."

Tyler took the paper and glanced at it. "I will see what I can do but I can't assure you that I can accomplish such a task."

"That's all Mr. Wake asks, that you see what you can do," replied Brace as he stood up, nodded at Kensie, and walked off.

"You're not planning on taking that assignment, are you?" asked Kensie.

"I'm not very excited about it. I don't even know if I can breathe in outer space, much less give a satellite going thousands of miles an hour a push."

"Then you're not going to attempt it?"

"I'll give it some thought and maybe do a test or two."

"I hope you plan to tell Dad about this."

"Yes, I will, but after my tests."

Kensie thought for a moment.

"Then you are going to do it?"

"Only if I find out I can," Tyler replied.

At dinner Kensie knew she couldn't bring up the subject about Brace and the request. That was Tyler's responsibility, but she found it hard not to say anything.

She was pleased that her mom and dad liked the outfit she'd bought and that made her feel better.

As for Tyler he had decided not to bring up either the window washer rescue or Mr. Wake's request. That could wait. So, he kept himself busy trying to see how much spaghetti he could fork into his mouth in one bite.

Chapter Nine

The Satellite

After dinner, Tyler went up early to his room. He needed to think and check on a few things. As he unfolded the paper Brace had handed him, he looked at the drawing of the navigational satellite he was supposed to fix and its instructions.

After scanning the satellite positioning information he decided to give his cousin Nicholas a call. Nicholas had told him that he'd written a paper about satellites for a physical science project.

"Hey, Nicholas. It's Tyler...Fine, how about you? ...Okay, good...well, a little...just a simple rescue from a tall building. I'll tell you guys about it when I see you next. When is next? I don't know, but soon, I hope. By the way, remember that paper you did on satellites you told me about? Could you get it? I have a couple of questions...Yeah, good. How high do satellites need to be in order to orbit?...Between 130 and 22,000 miles? You've got to be kidding...It depends upon the purpose for the satellite? Higher ones go around the earth every 24 hours or longer while lower ones go around in about 90 minutes. How about a satellite that helps ships to navigate? It's a lower satellite, about 150 miles up. And how fast would that be going? What! Over 17,000 miles an hour? You've got to be kidding!...Yeah, just wondering...No, I'm not going to do anything stupid. Just doing some basic research. Well thanks, Nicholas. See you soon."

"Wow," thought Tyler. *"I've never known how fast I can fly or if I can survive in outer space. But it looks like I'll need to test it out tonight. If I'm going to actually try to catch the satellite and push it faster, I'm probably going to have to do it during the day when I can both spot it in the sky and have the sun's energy."*

Tyler heard a knock on his bedroom door. He knew it would be Kensie.

"Come in, Kensie."

"Okay, so I suppose you're going to take a test run tonight, aren't you?"

"Whatever gave you that idea?"

"I know you really don't want to catch that satellite, but I'm sure you want to find out whether you have the ability to do it. Am I right?"

"You have spoken wisely," Tyler replied. "I knew you would."

"Then what would you do if you were me? Not find out the extent of your powers? Just sit and wonder? You know I need to figure all this out, figure out my limits and the ways I can be of service to Raul and possibly to Mr. Wake."

Kensie sat down on Tyler's bed. "You're right. I'd probably do the same thing. But I'm just concerned about you overdoing it and getting yourself hurt. I know you say you're indestructible, but it seems to me that all superheroes, like I said, have their Kryptonite."

"And maybe mine is outer space or a satellite traveling at 17,000 miles an hour?"

"Seventeen thousand miles an hour!" Kensie exclaimed.

"Yeah, give or take a thousand."

"You've got to be kidding me. I know you're fast but..."

"And that's what I've got to figure out. I know I can hold my breath under water a very long time and now I have to find out how I handle the lack of oxygen in space."

"So, when are you going to test it?"

"I'll need a little sunlight so I'll go up to the roof right about now," Tyler said as he headed towards the door.

"Hey Mom and Dad, I need to run a little errand. I'll be right back," Tyler yelled as he closed the front door and headed up to the roof where he would be out of sight if anyone was watching.

He looked around then focused on the sun that was beginning to set in the west over the beach. Although harder to see, the moon was hanging in the sky slightly above him. That should pull him into space...if it worked.

Tyler jumped towards the setting sun getting a full compliment of its energy and pull. Then he looked up at the moon and started climbing.

Before he glanced back at the earth, he'd already climbed high enough to see most of California's Central Coast and the Sierra Nevada Mountains to the east. He could feel the moon's pull and breathe in the fresh air within the clouds, but that soon gave way to shortened breath and lightness from the thinning oxygen.

"If I could hold my breath that long under water, I should be able to go without oxygen for some time in space," he thought.

The moon was still his energy source. As he left the gravitational pull of the earth, his speed increased. He leveled out by searching for bright stars above the earth's horizon. He was flying east in the direction the earth was spinning, but much faster.

Tyler knew that the earth spins in a twenty-four-hour cycle, rotating at one thousand miles an hour. He glanced at his watch and figured that if he held his speed for ninety minutes and circled the earth, his speed would have to be at least 17,000 miles per hour. That would be about the speed and height above the earth of the satellite he was supposed to catch. But could he hold his breath and keep up his speed for that length of time? So far it hadn't been a problem.

Soon he passed over America's east coast and headed across the Atlantic Ocean. England, then the European Continent appeared. As he continued east, he hoped he wouldn't become a target for a missile from Russia, then China, which he was flying over next. He was a small unidentified flying object, that must appear to be a satellite. At least that's what he hoped.

He glanced at his watch again and discovered he'd been flying for nearly an hour. He spotted Japan, below. He held his breath, but he didn't need to. Somehow, he didn't seem to need oxygen. So, he breathed in only to find that nothing filled his lungs and that seemed to be okay with his body.

He flew across the Pacific Ocean with the Hawaiian Islands barely visible below. A few minutes later the west coast of America appeared.

He began his decent into the Los Angeles area about eighty-five minutes into his flight. He realized that he'd flown faster than the satellite as he settled back down on his roof.

"Well, that was a long errand," said his mother when he came in the door. "You were gone almost an hour and a half."

"Sorry, I had to go a little further than I expected."

"If you want dessert there's ice cream in the fridge. We've already had some."

"Thanks, Mom, but I need to let you and Dad know what's happening. Do you both have a moment?"

"I heard you, Son," said his dad who'd been working on his computer at the kitchen table. "Come on over and we'll talk, or maybe just listen."

Just then Kensie entered the room after hearing Tyler's voice. Sydney followed behind her big sister.

"I want to update you all. Today on our walk to the Century Center one of Wake's associates named Brace stopped me and asked if I was going to accept Mr. Wake's proposal. I told him I would with the stipulations we'd talked about earlier. Later he found me and Kensie at the yogurt shop and told me that Mr. Wake needed a favor right away. I was surprised, but as he explained I understood why it was urgent."

"So, what was so urgent?" asked his dad.

"Apparently," Tyler continued, "Mr. Wake has shipping investments, and the satellite they use for navigation is about to break loose from its low orbit and fall to earth."

"So," said his mom.

"Because of its importance for shipping, he'd like me to...well...fly about one hundred and thirty miles into space, grab it, and push it into a faster and higher orbit."

Both his stunned parents looked at each other.

"And you declined?" asked his dad.

"Not exactly. I told him I'd think about it and see what I could do."

"That sounds extremely dangerous and beyond your abilities, at least as we understand them," replied his dad.

"Not really. I found out that in space I can fly faster than the Satellite's speed of over 17,000 miles per hour and can go to one hundred and thirty miles high without worrying about the oxygen."

"You what?" exclaimed his mother.

"Yeah, that was the little errand I had to run for the last hour and a half."

"So, you've just been in outer space?" asked his overwhelmed dad.

"You could say that, and it's a great view of the earth from up there. Besides, now I know about other powers I have."

His parents and sisters were quiet for some time before Kensie spoke up.

"Then you're planning on trying to catch a satellite and make it go higher and faster?"

"With what I've just learned it's worth a try. Besides it will save millions of dollars and possibly the lives of those who sail the ships that depend upon it."

"This seems to be getting out of control!" exclaimed his mother.

"Then what am I supposed to do with my powers? Ignore them and the people they can serve, or just forget I have them and go to school and be normal, which I'm not."

"Tyler," said his dad, "we know how difficult this is for you, so you have to understand how we feel too. This is all so sudden. Doing unbelievable acts that save people on earth is one thing, but now outer space?"

"Well, like I told Raul, I'll do anything he asks me to do within my ability. Now, Mr. Wake has also asked me to do something important and I think it's worth a try."

"We know it's your decision to make. So, if you're going to attempt it, when would that be?" asked his dad.

"Early tomorrow morning when the sun is just above the horizon so I can use its power and light to find the correct satellite."

"How are you ever going to find it?" asked his mother. "There have got to be hundreds of satellites in space?"

"Brace gave me all the information I'll need to find it...its height, speed, and its orbit, including a picture and the lettering, NAV 108, written on it. It also has a blinking light. With what seems to be my built-in GPS and great vision I should be able to find it.

Tyler went to bed earlier than usual. He knew he'd have trouble sleeping and he was right. He finally fell asleep around midnight but woke up at 5:30 a.m. He ate a light breakfast and again looked over the information Brace had given him about the satellite.

Kensie followed him up onto the roof just as the sun was hitting the tops of the trees.

"I know there is nothing I can say to change your mind," she said, "so, good luck."

"Thanks, I'll need it. If worse comes to worst, I'll be back shortly without adjusting the satellite. At least I would have tried."

With that said, Tyler jumped towards the morning sun.

Kensie could see him only for a moment as he disappeared into the sky.

Tyler knew that the satellite he sought would be orbiting overhead right about this time according to Brace's information. It would be traveling east to west at 17,400 miles per hour at one hundred and thirty miles high. From his flight and positioning yesterday he could pretty much estimate the height and speed he'd need in order to intercept it. He knew he had to search for the blinking light and unique solar wings that stuck out on all four sides, along with the NAV108 lettering.

At about sixty-two miles above earth he entered space and his speed began to increase. He leveled off at about 130 miles high and brought his speed up to the same 17,000 miles per hour speed he had held for over eighty minutes the day before. With his amazing vision he scanned the sky around him for a light blinking somewhere in the surrounding darkness.

Just below him he spotted a large object moving at his speed. He moved towards it hoping it was his target, but then noticed that it seemed to be a large piece of space junk from possibly an older satellite that had broken apart. He moved away from the large piece of metal and slightly increased his speed.

Again, he spotted something several hundred yards to his right that appeared to be spinning. As he approached it he realized that it must be a portion of a booster rocket that had been jettisoned from a spacecraft which had gone to orbit hundreds of miles above him.

"This is tough! There is a lot of junk up here besides satellites."

Then in the far distance he saw a light blinking. It seemed to be drawing him towards it.

"I hope this is coming from the satellite I've been looking for," he thought, as he headed towards the light.

For a moment, the light disappeared. And as he searched for it he noticed a distant speck below him flying much faster than he was going.

"That can't be it. It's many miles below me and traveling much too fast.

He knew he had to check it out so he focused on a lower star and headed down, way down. Strangely, the satellite seemed to glow brighter as he approached.

As he neared the object, he realized that it was the satellite he'd been looking for. He could clearly see the four solar wings extended around it. He was also able to identify the NAV108 lettering on its side as it sped by even though the lettering was hard to see due to the satellite's unexplained brightness.

"Great! It's traveling much too fast and seems to be increasing its speed every second. This thing must be losing its orbit super fast. If I'm not able to grab it soon, it might travel too fast and generate so much heat as it approaches the earth's atmosphere, that I won't be able to catch it or even touch it."

He forced himself to find a larger star in the direction of the satellite to increase his light power and speed. He finally saw one and strained to catch up. He was approaching faster than he wanted and knew he had just a split second to grab hold of one of the solar wings. He hoped, when he did, the wing wouldn't snap off

"Man, this is like catching a fly ball in center field while running twenty thousand miles an hour! I hope I can correctly estimate my speed compared to the satellite's," he thought as he prepared for the catch.

He clasped his hand around one of the solar panels.

Within a couple of seconds, he was zooming towards it flying way too fast. He cupped his hand and tried to avoid hitting it. One mistake and he could either smash into it possibly destroying it, or miss completely. Then he would have to try again if it didn't increase in speed beyond his ability to catch up with it.

Tyler felt a sudden jerk of his arm and body as he clasped his hand around the blade of one of the solar arms. He held on with all his super power as both he and the satellite continued to move forward at an even faster speed.

Tyler could see that the satellite had dropped so low that the gravitational pull of the earth countered its orbit and was pulling it directly into the earth's atmosphere. He knew he'd have to act fast before the satellite continued to descend and start burning up.

He quickly looked for the sun as he pulled himself around to the directional front of the satellite, now pointed right at him, but in this position he faced the sun. Both hands pushed against the satellite as he felt the sun's full force of energy ignite his body. The satellite gradually began to slow to the point where Tyler soon had control of it.

Tired, but pleased, Tyler knew he needed to take the satellite up to at least one hundred and fifty miles and possibly a bit higher to regain its original orbit. At that elevation its speed should be 17,400 thousand miles per hour. Within a few minutes he knew he had achieved his goal and the satellite should stay at that position and speed for years to come.

As the satellite sped off, Tyler felt especially proud of himself. Still he couldn't believe that this all began a few weeks ago when he'd felt some strange energy in his body. Now he'd just literally caught a speeding satellite in outer space and was flying home for breakfast. Go figure!

His mom and sisters were waiting in the kitchen. His dad was preparing to leave for work.

"Wow, you sure had all of us worrying," said his mom as she gave him a hug.

"Me too," added Kensie.

"Me three," chimed in Sydney.

Tyler couldn't help but smile.

"Just another day at work," he said as he grabbed a bowl and poured some cereal into it.

"Well?" said Kensie.

Tyler knew what she meant so he chewed and talked at the same time as he gave them a blow by blow description of his trip to outer space.

Within the hour the phone rang. Sydney picked it up.

"Hello, yes, just a moment. It's for you," she said as she handed it to Tyler.

"Hello," he said. For the next minute or so he just listened. "Yes, I appreciate that...bye."

"Who was that?" his mom asked.

"That was Mr. Wake. He said that he doesn't often use the phone, but in this case, he had to. He told me that he was extremely pleased by what I'd accomplished and that the satellite was now back in a position to save many lives. Millions of dollars can now be used for other important things. He said that he owed me big time and that he'd ask for my help again only if it was truly necessary."

"That was nice of him," said his mom.

"Yeah, I'm a little surprised at it. I had him figured for someone I might not be able to trust. He even gave me his personal telephone number. I still need to be cautious, but he might not be as bad as I thought he was."

Chapter Ten

FBI and Space Mountain

After Tyler's trip into space, he and Kensie worked on some projects for the High School Planning Committee to Welcome Freshman. They made handouts of all the clubs and activities of their school and invited the new students to join. They also decorated some of the "Welcome Bags" for goodies the Committee members were going to pass out.

"These are both good ideas," said Tyler. "Sorry I missed the first meeting."

"It's okay, but remember the next one is the day after tomorrow," reminded Kensie.

"And tomorrow, Sydney, you and I meet our cousins at Disneyland!"

"Wow, I almost forgot. I need to remind Dad that he needs to drive us there tomorrow," replied Tyler.

"You know, Tyler, you could just pick me up and fly us over if Mom and Dad are using the cars."

"Let's not go there, Kensie. Besides, where would we land and not be seen, on top of the Matterhorn?" asked Tyler.

"Yeah, I see what you mean."

Tyler's dad said he was free to drive him, Kensie, and Sydney across town to Disneyland to meet their cousins. They all had season passes which made it easier for them and actually brought the cost down quite a bit if they went there several times a year.

"This is going to be fun," said Sydney. "I like hanging out with Nicholas, Jonathan, and Mikaia, especially in Disneyland."

"Me too," replied Tyler as he found a parking spot.

When they approached the entrance Kensie said, "They'll meet us just inside the gate. Matter of fact," she continued as she flashed her pass to the ticket taker, "I see them now."

"Hi! Glad we were all able to get together again so soon!" said Mikaia as she walked toward her cousins.

"Yeah," added Jonathan. "This is one of my favorite places and we always have fun together here."

"Even though we're getting a little too old for some of the stuff here, I definitely still enjoy it," said Nicholas.

"I guess we're all just little kids at heart," replied Kensie.

"And, besides everything else, I hope a part of us will always stay that way," added Tyler.

"By the way," said Nicholas, "you need to bring us up to date about your latest exploits. Kensie said something on the phone about you flying into space."

"Something like that, but I'll fill you in as we look around and stand in lines," Tyler replied.

"I don't know about you, but I didn't take time for breakfast this morning so I'm hungry," said Jonathan.

"So am I," added Nicholas.

"Then let's stop at the Main Street eatery and grab something," suggested Mikaia.

"I'm game," said Tyler as they turned and headed into the Town Square and down Main Street.

They found the small eatery and sat down. Most of them ordered a sandwich while Jonathan ordered a hamburger. The cousins were anxious to hear about what Tyler had been doing so he enjoyed sharing his last few exploits with them. Nicholas especially couldn't believe Tyler had flown into outer space to re-orbit a satellite.

"So that's what your phone call was about? Information gathering for a project for Mr. Wake?"

As Nicholas spoke, two men in dark suits suddenly appeared.

"Sorry to interrupt, but aren't you Tyler Frazier?" they asked looking at Tyler.

Tyler, not too surprised, replied, "Yes, I'm Tyler. What can I do for you?"

"First, we're not Disneyland security. We're from the FBI," the sandy blond-haired man replied flipping out his badge.

Everyone just stared at Tyler to see what he was going to do next.

"We need to speak with you," the man continued.

"And what does this have to do with?" Tyler asked.

"We'd prefer to speak with you in private," he replied.

"Well, these are my cousins and sisters. Anything you ask me is fine for them to hear."

"Don't make it awkward for everyone. We know who they are. What we have to talk to you about comes under the articles of national security. We need to speak to you in private."

"First, how did you know I was here?"

"We were alerted when you first ran your pass through the electronic reader at the front gate."

"Then you've been watching me?" Tyler asked.

"We'll just say that you've come to our attention recently. We have access to a back-office room just across the square. Would you follow us, please?"

"Yes, but I want a witness to this, I guess, interview, so I'd like my sister, Kensie to come with us."

"That doesn't sound like it's ..."

"If it's not possible," Tyler interrupted, "then you'll have to arrest me and since I'm under age, call my parents, who in turn would call our lawyer."

"There is actually no need for that," the same agent replied. "We just want to ask you a few questions. If you like, your sister may come."

"Why don't you guys go ahead? I don't know how long this will take. When we're done, I'll call you and we can meet up," said Tyler as he and Kensie stood up and followed behind the agents.

The agents opened an unobtrusive side door into a building, entered, and walked down a hallway. After passing several doors, they entered a small conference room with ten chairs around a rectangular table.

"Have a seat please. I'm Agent Ferrell and this is Agent Gerard. Like I said, we'd like to ask you a few questions about your recent activities."

"Fine with me," replied Tyler.

"Two rather unusual things have happened lately in the Century City area near your home that have come to the attention of the local police," said Agent Ferrell.

"What are you referring to?" Tyler asked.

Agent Ferrell looked at Tyler for a second, obviously to see his reaction before continuing.

"One was a three-car accident on Pico. The other was an ambulance turning over on Olympic Boulevard. In both cases witnesses said that a young man saved the lives of several people by interceding."

"What did the witnesses say he did?" Tyler asked.

"During the Pico accident he pushed a car off a second burning car, pulled the door off, and took out the two people trapped inside. On Olympic he actually seemed to catch the ambulance that was turning over and cushioned its fall thereby saving the two ambulance personnel inside."

"Wow, I find that hard to believe," said Tyler. "Was he hurt?"

"According to the witnesses, apparently not, because he quickly disappeared into the crowd."

"So, who was he?" Tyler asked. "Did anyone get a good look at him?"

Agent Gerard, who had been carefully watching and listening to Tyler, decided to get involved.

"Actually," agent Gerard noted, "no one seems to have gotten a good look at him but they say that he was a kid, about your age and height, with brown hair."

"So why do you think I had anything to do with these events? I remember reading about them in the paper, especially since they happened so close to our home, but that's all. And why would this interest the FBI?"

"Yesterday," continued Agent Gerard, "we were contacted by the CIA regarding another strange event, one that took place in space. It had to do with a satellite that suddenly increased its orbit as well as an object that was spotted coming from Century City."

"Then that is very strange," replied Tyler. "But what does this have to do with me?"

"From what the CIA was able to assess, that object seemed to come and go from the roof of your building," replied Agent Gerard as both agents closely watched Tyler.

"Wow! Are they sure that this object came from my building?"

"Reasonably sure. But it was a small object which was moving very fast."

"Now I understand why you're interested. But what does this have to do with me?"

"It is because of these several coincidences that happened near you. Besides the fact that we checked the last U.S. Census Report and found out that to our knowledge, you're the only young man of that approximate age, height, and description who lives in this building,"

"That's fine, but the last census report was done five years ago. Have you checked this building and others nearby for someone else that may match that description?" Tyler asked.

"No, we've not gone to that extreme yet but it looks like we may have to," Agent Gerard replied.

"We were hoping you could shed some light on these occurrences and who this mystery person could be or at least what exactly the object was that was tracked by the CIA," interjected Agent Ferrell.

"I'm afraid I can't help you much on all of that. I've been in and out and very busy getting ready for school, but I will keep my eyes open. I was also quite interested in the two accidents that took place near us a few days ago."

Both agents sat still for a few moments as Tyler and Kensie watched them.

Suddenly, Agent Ferrell stood up followed by Agent Gerald.

"Then that will be all, for now. We appreciate your time and cooperation. We'll walk you out. You and your cousins have a great day at Disneyland."

"Man, that was intense," said Kensie as Tyler pulled out his cell phone.

"Yeah, you can say that again. Now I have to be extra careful knowing they'll be watching me. I'll need to fill Dad and Raul in on this when we get home. As for now, we're in Disneyland, so let's have some fun."

Tyler's call found their cousins and Kensie and Sydney in line at Space Mountain, one of Mikaia's favorite rides.

"Hi, so Mikaia's the Space Mountain girl," Tyler said as they approached their sisters and cousins.

"I am. And I really like that it's dark and you don't know what's going to happen next," Mikaia replied.

"How about you, Tyler?" asked Nicholas. "What did they want?"

"Looks like they're beginning to catch on to some of the things I've been up to. Because of the nearby accidents and descriptions, along with something moving back and forth into space near our building, they think I may have something to do with it. They're only speculating, but I'll need to watch my back from now on."

"Looks like our intelligence agencies are in fact rather intelligent," noted Jonathan, "especially since they're right."

"That's what I was thinking too," replied Tyler. "I'll have to think of more covert ways to use my powers."

"Hey, it's almost our turn," said an excited Mikaia. "I get to sit in the front!"

"And I get to sit in the front with you!" shouted Kensie.

"And I'll be behind you two!" joined in Sydney.

"We'll take the next one," said Nicholas who was trying to adjust his favorite camera in order to take pictures in the dark.

Into the darkness headed Mikaia, Kensie, Sydney, and several others.

"I'm in the front on this one!" exclaimed Jonathan.

"And I'll ride shotgun," replied Nicholas.

By the time Tyler had moved towards the coaster only the back seat was left.

"Then I'll take the back seat!" he shouted out as though that was the seat he really wanted.

Off they shot into the dark. Instantly Tyler could see inside the whole structure of Space Mountain. It was a maze of steel tracks and support beams set at all angles and positions. He could clearly see the coasters as they moved rapidly around the tracks as screams echoed through the metal structure.

Tyler heard a faint sound of metal scrapping metal. It became louder at every turn. He looked at the coaster in which Mikaia, Kensie, and Sydney were riding and detected a few slightly noticeable sparks spraying off the tracks below.

He focused on the runners below the coaster noticing that the two in front were wobbling. He realized that if those broke loose the rest of the runners would follow them off the tracks thus taking the entire coaster with them.

Tyler kept focused on the track. Since it was pitch black no one else had any idea what could happen. The loud screams continued as Tyler hoped the front coaster would make it all the way around. Then he'd say something to the attendants.

Unfortunately, that didn't happen. At the very next sharp turn the front runners broke loose leading the coaster off the track and into the dark.

Tyler could hear the screams of Mikaia, Kensie, and Sydney as they suddenly realized what was happening. But their screams were only mixed in with all the others.

Tyler knew he must act fast. By luck or maybe by fate he was sitting in the back seat of his coaster. No one would see him make his move.

He jumped and flew in the direction of the plummeting coaster. He positioned himself under the front. Realizing that he'd never be able to get it back on the tracks with the broken runners, he gently helped it glide to the floor under the coaster structure. By then an alarm had sounded. All the coasters slowed to a stop as he shot back up to his seat as the inside of Space Mountain lit up.

The screams continued as most people were unaware of what had happened and found themselves stuck in coasters at various locations. Gradually security personnel and attendants came in with various ladders and lifts with which to unload the passengers from the coasters.

Several had gathered around Mikaia, Kensie, and Sydney's coaster. Some people were checking them all out to make sure they were all right. Others were asking them questions about the coaster and what had happened.

Tyler could make out most of what they were saying. He heard the words 'miracle' and 'unbelievable' spoken several times. The words 'lucky' and 'guardian angel' were also used. Tyler was just very glad that he'd been there and that he was sitting in the last seat of the coaster behind them. If not, the accident would have taken a much more serious turn for Mikaia and his sisters. He realized that maybe that was part of the reason for his new powers. He knew he must use them for good and helping others, but this event brought it even closer to home for him. He also wondered why all these things kept happening around him.

After about an hour the cousins joined up with each other outside of Space Mountain.

"Man, that was exciting!" exclaimed Jonathan.

"Yeah, maybe for you but not for us," said Mikaia.

"We were almost killed when our coaster broke loose from the tracks!" added Kensie.

"And by the way, Tyler, thanks. We're sure glad you had our backs!" stated Sydney.

"How do you know I had anything to do with it?"

Nicholas looked at Tyler, put his arm on his shoulder, and said, "Then it must have been one of those super FBI agents who followed you into the mountain. They probably thought you were too busy and had used the darkness of the mountain to fly off for an adventure elsewhere."

"Actually, Tyler, we are very grateful for your quick action," said Mikaia.

Tyler smiled and quietly said, "If I can't help my sisters and cousins out once in a while, what good are these powers?"

"By the way," said Jonathan, "I have this geometry test on Friday and with your new brain power you could..."

"Wrong kind of help!" Tyler quickly added as they all laughed.

"I am concerned that the agents may still be in the park watching me. If they heard about the 'miracle' in the mountain and knew I was there too, it could point a finger right at me!"

"Well, right now let's take some more rides including The Pirates of the Caribbean and maybe eat in the Blue Bayou Restaurant," suggested Jonathan.

"Thinking with your stomach again, Jonathan. I like it!" said Kensie.

The rest of the day the cousins had a great time enjoying the rides as well as the various snack areas. Each of them kept an eye out for the agents, hoping they had left and weren't investigating the Space Mountain accident.

When Tyler and his sisters arrived home, their mom told them that Raul had called and left his number for Tyler. So, Tyler went to his room and called him.

After a few minutes Tyler came out.

"And what was that all about?" his mom asked.

"Raul had heard about my latest flight into space from some unnamed sources and wanted to know what it was all about. I told him about Mr. Wade and Brace and what they'd asked me to do. I told him what had happened and what I was able to achieve with the satellite. He felt that I'd done the right thing and was quite impressed by my abilities to accomplish such a difficult assignment.

"I also told him about the FBI interviewing me today at Disneyland and about their suspicions."

"They did what?" his mother asked.

Tyler had forgotten to tell his mom about the interview so he spent a moment filling her in.

"It seems that you'll have to be very careful about how you go about any assignment you choose to accept," she replied.

"Yeah, for one I'll need to take off just above the trees so any radar or detection devices won't be able to identify me until I'm well away from home.

Chapter Eleven

Followed and a Freighter

The next morning Tyler and Kensie headed to their high school to attend the second meeting of the Committee to Welcome Freshman. They both wore their backpacks which contained the handouts they had made and the decorated welcome bags they had put together. Unfortunately, their parents needed to use both cars.

"When do you think we're going to buy a third car? This walking everywhere is inefficient," said Tyler.

"It's funny you'd bring that up since you can fly around the world in ninety minutes," replied Kensie.

"Maybe that's why it bothers me so much when I could get to Disneyland or school in a few seconds."

"Well, I can't drive yet so maybe Mom and Dad are waiting 'til then to buy another car," said Kensie.

"I hope it's sooner than that. I'll be going to college in two years and I don't want to have to rely on my flying abilities to get me back and forth to class. However, the good news is if I were attending a college on the east coast, like Princeton, I could still live at home and save the cost of housing while simply flying over and back each day," added Tyler with a big grin.

I noticed a cream-colored Ford about a half block away.

"Yeah, the FBI would never figure that one out!" replied Kensie.

Tyler suddenly slowed down.

"Hey, what did you see," asked Kensie, "a basketball hoop in someone's yard you wanted to dunk a ball into?"

"No, but that's not a bad idea since basketball is my favorite sport. I noticed a cream-colored Ford about a half block away, which has turned the last four corners with us. I believe Agents Ferrell and Gerard could be on the prowl."

Kensie started to turn to take a look when Tyler instantly touched her shoulder.

"Don't turn around. They may be watching us with binoculars. I don't want them to think we've spotted them. That way we'll have more of a chance to lose them when we want to."

"Sorry about that, but I wish those two would get a life," replied Kensie as they both sped up.

"Now I know how it feels to be a deer hunted by a couple of guys with guns," she added.

When they arrived at school everyone on the committee was there and had completed the tasks assigned to them. Tyler felt good about that since he'd worked with others before who liked being on committees where everyone else did all the work.

A few more tasks were assigned and after a little pep talk by the advising teacher, Mrs. Shawn, they were on their way home.

Tyler and Kensie stopped and peeked out a window near the front door.

"Now do you see it?" Tyler said as he pointed down the block to a cream-colored car parked along the street.

"Yep, Ferrell and Gerard probably sitting there munching on donuts."

"Do you want to have some fun?" asked Tyler.

"Me, have fun? Of course not, but whatever it is let's do it."

"Then we'll sneak around the back of the school, jog along the bushes next to the baseball field, duck under the bleachers and head down the street leading to the Century Center Mall. That will make them stop chewing."

"I'm right behind you, only don't jog too fast," Kensie replied.

Within a few minutes they were both at the yogurt shop choosing their favorite flavors and toppings.

"I bet they're still sitting at the school waiting for us to come out. Maybe they'll figure it out when the custodians turn off the lights tonight," laughed Tyler.

"I wouldn't want to make them late to bed," added Kensie.

"Actually, they probably sleep in their car when they're on stake-outs," replied Tyler.

"You think they're watching our home 24/7?" asked Kensie.

"Only if they really feel I'm the one they're looking for. Let's check it out tonight and see how serious they are about me."

That night, just after dark, Tyler and Kensie made their way down the stairs to the alley behind their building. They followed the alley down two blocks then snuck out to the front street and took a look. Tyler, of course, could easily see down the street in the dark of night.

"I don't see their car or anyone actually sitting in a car in case they switched with other agents for the night," reported Tyler.

"You don't think they're still parked at the school?"

"I really don't think they're that incompetent," Tyler replied. "So, if agents aren't watching for me at night, then they're probably still speculating about me being someone of interest, and that's good to know."

As soon as Tyler and Kensie came back into their home, Tyler's dad told him to call Raul who had just phoned.

"Apparently it's very urgent. Looks like you may have another assignment," said his dad.

"When does a young superhero get a couple of days off," Tyler asked as his father patted him on the back.

"I guess never when you have a unique skill and there is great demand and a tiny supply. That's capitalism, besides what else would you be doing?"

"I could watch the Dodgers versus the Giants baseball game that's on right now," he replied.

"Well, whatever Raul wants you'll probably be back shortly so I'll record it for you."

"Thanks Dad, but maybe on my way back I'll just land there and watch the game from the cheap seats."

"In that case here's twenty dollars."

"What's that for? I can probably get in free."

"Just in case you're hungry that will buy you a hot dog and a soda. Food at ball parks isn't cheap."

"Thanks, Dad, but now I'd better call Raul."

A moment later Tyler came out of his room.

"So, what's up?" asked Kensie.

"This is a new one for me. A freighter bound for the Philippines from Hawaii is caught in a major storm about half way there. The storm had caused the large shipping containers on the deck of the ship to shift. The ship is listing to its port side and could tip over at any moment. Apparently, there are no other ships in the area and the weather makes a rescue by air impossible."

"So why has Raul been contacted about it?" asked his mother.

"The cargo on the ship is all medical and emergency supplies that the Red Cross is shipping to the Philippines, the distributing center for the south eastern Pacific. These supplies are very expensive and badly needed. Besides, there is a crew of twenty-five on board who'd probably not survive in the small life boats in the heavy sea if they had to abandon ship."

"And what are you supposed to do?" asked his dad.

"Apparently I'm supposed to upright the ship by moving the shipping containers to center again before it tips over."

"Then I guess you'd better hurry," said his dad.

"And be careful!" yelled his mom as Tyler headed out the door.

Even though Tyler didn't think the agents were watching, he went back down the stairs and followed the alley up the hill for three blocks. Then he jumped toward a bright low star in the western sky and stayed just above the trees to speed out over the Pacific.

From there he gained some altitude as he thought about the navigational information directing him to the ship that Raul had given him. He laughed to himself when Raul had mentioned that the GPS information guiding him would be directed off the very satellite he had pushed back into orbit two days earlier.

"Go figure," he thought.

As he flew across the Pacific towards the setting sun just south of the Hawaiian Islands, he noticed that the darkness was getting lighter. He realized that he was traveling much faster than the earth could turn. He knew that he would need that extra energy from the sunlight when he arrived at the storm since the heavy rain and clouds would block out any light source energy for him to use.

He soon spotted the massive storm below him and figured out where the ship would be located. If the ship still had power, the Captain would have every light turned on in case there was any chance that someone could answer their distress call. If not, Tyler knew he'd have to depend on his super vision to find it.

As he dove down into the storm, he realized just how destructive it would be if it hit the mainland. Even with his power he had some difficulty flying straight as the hundred miles an hour winds pushed against him.

Fortunately, the positioning information from Raul had been correct and the ship still had power. He spotted the ship after circling around just a couple of times.

He could see that at the angle it was listing it could roll over at any moment. The shipping containers on the deck had shifted over to the port side. There were four rows six high and three wide on the front and three rows stacked the same on the stern.

Because there was so much wind and rain, Tyler determined that the crew would be unable to see him even from the Pilot House.

He flew down to the first stack of containers near the bow and pushed them back toward the center. Since the other six stacks were still leaning, they immediately began sliding back to the port side. One stack at a time wasn't enough to stop the ship from listing on its side.

For a moment Tyler thought that his task was impossible. Then he noticed the tall cargo boom just behind the navigational tower. Quickly, he flew over to it and discovered that it was made of a heavy metal. If he could break it loose and use it like a plow to push three stacks of containers at a time back to center, maybe that would shift enough weight to bring the ship upright.

Putting his shoulder against the boom, he flew as hard as he could into it. He was glad that he had been flying into the setting sun and had had the opportunity to power up on its rays. Within few seconds the boom broke loose causing a loud metal screech like someone scratching his fingers across a chalkboard. He brought it around and was able to use it to push against three stacks of containers at once. As he did the ship slowly shifted back towards center.

Tyler laid the boom back down on the deck and quickly pushed each of the other stacks back into place. Then he used the boom to brace the first three stacks so they couldn't shift again in the heavy seas.

As Tyler flew back over the Pacific Ocean, he checked his watch and realized that the whole assignment had taken only forty minutes. The Dodgers Baseball game would still be on. He decided to stop and take in the last few innings of the game. With everyone still watching the game, the parking lot would be empty of people, so he decided to land there, then hop the fence, and climb up the stairs to the cheap seats.

"There are always a couple of those unfilled," Tyler thought.

Sure enough, the stadium was lit up and the parking lot was virtually empty, so he flew down and landed between two of the twenty buses that were parked next to the back gate entrance.

Since the game was more than half over, Tyler didn't feel guilty about bounding over the fence and walking up the stairs to the highest seats. As he reached into his pocket, he found the twenty dollars his dad had given to him. He smiled as he rubbed it against his fingers. He headed down a few rows and into the stadium to one of the concession stands and bought the hot dog and soda he'd been thinking about since his dad had mentioned them to him. Then he climbed back up and found an empty seat to watch the last four innings of the game.

Tyler left just before the game ended with the Dodgers ahead five to three. He needed to get back to the parking lot and take off before the crowd began to leave.

He climbed back over the fence, checked for anyone that might be watching, located a star, and jumped into the sky. He kept his flight low, just above the trees and of course the tall buildings.

Within a few seconds he landed in the alley three buildings beyond his and then ran to the back stairs and into his home.

"That was quick," said his dad when Tyler sat down at the kitchen table.

"Yeah, a big storm and I got drenched with rain, but I dried off as I flew," he replied.

"Then were you able to save the ship and crew?" asked Kensie.

"I got it upright and then secured the containers so most of them wouldn't shift again in the storm, but the rest is up to the Captain and crew. I guess I could have tried to pick up the massive ship and fly it away from the storm, but I believe that would have been beyond the scope of my powers. I'm sure the crew is trained to deal with storms if the ship stays upright."

"Gosh, Tyler," said Kensie. "It's almost unimaginable that you're doing such amazing things, then simply flying back home for dinner. I find myself asking you questions I wouldn't ever be able to ask anyone else. Hey Tyler, what was your day like? Oh, I just saved a ship full of people, a mine full of trapped miners, my cousin from a Tiger, and a satellite in outer space. Other than that, my day's been rather boring!"

"When you put it that way, Kensie, it does sound rather unbelievable," replied Tyler, "but I'm kind of getting used to it."

"Just remember, school starts in just a couple of weeks," said his mom, "and I expect you to concentrate on your studies. You do want to go on to college and get a good education and job, don't you?"

Kensie, Sydney, and Dad looked over at Christina and grinned.

Finally, Tyler spoke.

"Yes, Mom, of course I do, but don't you think what Kensie just said my day was like would be a pretty good job to pursue? Much less the fact that if I need any information at all I just have to think about it and it's there."

Christina paused for a moment and said, "Now that you mention it that did sound rather silly, didn't it?"

Everyone nodded.

"But you are right. I do want to enjoy just being a kid in high school and college. Besides, it's a good cover for me and my powers, you know being just a school boy."

Raul called and thanked Tyler for his quick action on saving the freighter. He wanted to know exactly what Tyler was able to do and how things turned out. Of course, Tyler was delighted to talk to someone besides his family about it. Raul still couldn't believe what a godsend Tyler was to their relief efforts. With each assignment he was able to stop a disaster before relief help was even sent.

Tyler went to bed for the first time that night feeling pretty good about himself and what he'd been able to accomplish. He realized he still had a lot to learn about his powers and the responsibilities that went with them.

However, now his main concern was to answer questions like: Why me? Where did these powers come from and how long will they last? If they last forever, did that mean he'd live forever too?

As Tyler thought about living forever his body began to shiver, for that had even more implications for him and his family. But despite his concerns he was soon asleep. Apparently even he, Energized Man, needed some sleep.

Chapter Twelve

Gary, Ferrell, and Gerard

The next morning Tyler had made arrangements with a couple of his friends to meet at school to play basketball. He'd known these five guys for several years, and they had often gotten together to play during the school year. They didn't meet up that much in the summer since most of them had summer jobs or were away on vacations with their families. Tyler always loved a good basketball game.

Tyler jogged all the way to school carrying his favorite basketball. It was an open gym so a couple of his friends arrived early to make sure they got a court. As he looked over his shoulder, he noticed a cream-colored car about a half block away. He simply smiled to himself and sped up a bit.

His friends had commented several times on how much he'd improved over the last few months. Even the varsity coach had told him he wanted Tyler on the team. Because Tyler knew something strange was happening to him, he had shied away from joining the team. He had felt that it wouldn't be fair to the other teams they played.

So Tyler knew he needed to keep things under control and only made a few amazing moves and shots. Even then he was pleased to hear his friends comment on how great he was. He had had little opportunity for anyone to compliment him on all the unbelievable things he'd actually accomplished recently.

After the game he and his friend Gary bought sodas from a mini store near the school and then sat down at an outside table to talk.

Tyler had known that Gary was worried about losing his home in Century City since his father didn't have enough money to pay the mortgage. Gary had told him he might have to move soon and leave their school.

"If you don't mind me asking, what does your dad do?" Tyler asked.

"Well, he used to work in the marine salvage business for a large company. He thought that if he went off on his own, he'd be more successful. He actually found a sunken ship from the late 1850's that was taking gold mined in California to Washington D.C. just before the outbreak of the Civil War. Only he knows the location, and he planned on recovering it. He put everything we had into the salvaging project. He said it would be by far his biggest and most valuable salvage operation and if he succeeded, we would be set for life."

"What happened?" asked Tyler.

"So he bought all the equipment he needed for a deep savage operation and hired an experienced crew. Unfortunately, he's still out beyond the Channel Islands off the coast trying to bring up the cargo, which of course is the gold. But everything isn't working right and he's run out of money and has to return all the equipment in the next few days."

"I'm sorry to hear that, Gary."

"Yeah, no one will lend us any more money. At the same time, he can't free the winch and scoop he was using because it's stuck several hundred feet down. So, in three days we'll have no money and a bunch of loans we can't pay."

"Do you know where your dad is?" Tyler asked.

"Sort of, but he's kept secret the exact location. I do know he's about twenty-five miles west of Santa Rosa Island."

"Wow! That's sad. I feel really bad for you, especially since your dad's put so much work into all of that!" replied Tyler.

"That's just the way things are, but I will miss school and our games a lot."

"Hang in there. Maybe something will come up."

"We've been praying about it, but I don't think it's going to happen," said Gary.

"Will you be able to play next week or...."

"I don't know, but I hope so."

"Then we'll save a spot for you just in case," said Tyler.

"Thanks," said Gary.

On his way home, with the cream-colored car still following, Tyler couldn't stop thinking about Gary's situation. He had known him for several years and they had planned to graduate together. He wished he could help in some way, but what could he do? He didn't have any money.

"Hi, Tyler," said Kensie as he came through the door. "Are those agents still following you?"

"They've got to get a life, or at least drive a different colored car sometimes."

"So how was the game?" she asked.

"Great, but we may lose one of our players."

"That's too bad. Who is it?"

"Gary."

"Not Gary! Why?" Kensie asked.

"Money!"

"Okay, but why?"

"His dad has put everything they own into a sea salvage operation of an 1850's ship that sunk with a cargo of gold. They've run out of time and money and some of their equipment is stuck on the bottom of the ocean."

"What's he going to do?"

"There is nothing either of them can do, but according to Gary they'll need to move soon."

"Can't they borrow?"

"No one else will lend to them. I wish I could help, but I don't have any money," said Tyler.

Kensie thought for a moment.

"Gary is a good friend of yours, isn't he?"

"Yes."

"Then how long can you hold your breath?"

"What does that have to do with anything?" asked Tyler.

"Under water, that is," replied Kensie.

Tyler knew what Kensie was thinking.

"Then you think I should try to dive down hundreds feet into the ocean and see if I can break loose the scoop that's stuck?"

"So, you did fly 130 miles out into space. The water thing should be easy, well, maybe easy," replied Kensie.

"I'm not sure. I think I could probably do it, but should I be using my powers for various friends for their economic gain?" Tyler asked. "This isn't life or death, but a bad business decision."

"I know and only you can answer that question. But then again, a little help from a friend once in a while is usually a good thing," added Kensie.

Tyler thought for a moment.

"Okay, I'll see what I can do, but not until sunset. His dad's boat and crew will still be out there if their scoop is stuck to the ocean bottom, so I'll need to be careful I'm not seen," Tyler replied.

As the sun was setting Tyler once again ran up the ally before he launched himself into the air. Since Gary's father's salvage boat was west of the Santa Rosa Island just off the California coast, it would take him just a couple of minutes to get there but maybe longer to find the boat. He did know that larger ships would still be sailing at night but that smaller ones, like the salvage boat, should be back in their harbors. So, he needed to look for a salvage boat, with a big winch on it, which looked like it was anchored and not moving.

Tyler finally jumped into the setting sun and quickly flew just above the buildings and trees. He was a bit annoyed that he had to be so careful now that Agents Ferrell and Gerard were following him around. He hoped they'd find something better to do.

Soon Tyler was flying over Santa Rosa Island and heading west for twenty-five miles. He spotted a couple of freighters sailing north but couldn't make out any smaller boats. He circled high expanding his search distance each time he completed a circle.

The fourth time around Tyler caught sight of a forty-foot boat with a winch and several lights turned on.

"This must be it," he thought, as he strained to see if the winch had a cable extended down into the water.

Sure enough, the cable was extended, probably with the deep-water scoop caught on the ocean's bottom thus anchoring the boat right where it was.

Tyler decided to drop into the water about fifty yards behind the boat. He held his breath and headed down the cable. If he caught hold of it and followed it down, even in the darkness, he would end up where the scoop was caught.

Deeper and deeper he went. Now any light was gone and darkness surrounded him, but somehow, he was still able to see. After a couple minutes he made out an old ship that was lying on the bottom. Its wooden frame and masts reminded him of old shipwrecks that he'd seen on the Discovery Channel.

Tyler noted that the scoop had apparently shattered the side of the ship and was now caught in the middle. As he pulled away old timbers and dirt, he spotted a golden gleam. He brushed away more dirt and could see that the scoop was partly embedded in a mound of gold bars.

"Man!" he thought, *"Gary's dad was right on. Not only was there gold but he put the scoop right on it! He was literally a scoop away from paying all his bills!"*

An excited Tyler realized that finding this gold meant Gary could stay in school and not have to move. To make sure of that Tyler not only broke the scoop loose, but loaded as much gold into it as it could safely hold. The rest of the gold he stacked up.

He then moved more timbers aside to make it an easy target for the next scoop drop.

Tyler was aware that he needed to let Gary's dad know that the scoop was free, so he decided to pull on the cable several times, thus moving the boat up and down. He hoped the motion would show that the scoop had broken loose from whatever was holding it.

Sure enough, a few seconds later he could see the cable tighten as the winch slowly lifted its precious cargo towards the surface.

With that he swam up and away from the boat and flew into the half-moon sky.

Now Tyler realized that once in a while it was okay to use his powers to help a friend.

Tyler arrived home for a late dinner. His family had waited to eat until his return. As he devoured the spaghetti and Caesar Salad that his mom had made, he enjoyed sharing with them all that he had been able to do.

Just as Tyler's mom brought out the apple crisp for dessert, the phone rang.

"Man!" said Kensie. "What bad timing! The dessert's just arrived!"

His dad answered the phone.

"Ah, Tyler, it's for you. It's Raul."

Tyler took a deep breath, and then moved towards the phone.

"How am I going to be able to go to school and do what other kids do with all these things taking place?" he asked as he picked up the phone.

"Raul...yeah, we're just finishing. ...No, that's okay, go ahead. ...Tomorrow morning at 9:00 am? Sure, I can be there."

"Well?" asked his dad.

"He wants to meet with me in the morning and fill me in on several possible problems."

"Actually, Tyler," said Kensie, "if you were getting paid for this, you would be able to live on your retirement money by now."

"You think so? Then I better ask for a raise tomorrow."

"I didn't think you were getting paid by the Council," said his mom.

"That is true," Tyler replied.

"Then a raise from something that's nothing makes it nothing. Am I right?" asked Kensie.

Tyler scratched his head and replied, "That about summarizes it I'm afraid."

They all began to laugh.

"So," said Tyler as he took a seat the next morning in Raul's office after a friendly greeting by Raul and his staff, "you have some possible assignments you would like to discuss with me?"

"I did until another matter came up," replied Raul.

"And what would that be?"

"The two FBI agents, Ferrell and Gerard visited me late yesterday. They've apparently been watching my office too. Between your visits and some interesting activities in the area and world, they seem to feel that, somehow, we may be involved. They know what I do and placing you with me, they've jumped to some conclusions."

Now Raul had Tyler's complete attention.

"Then they are a lot smarter than I gave them credit for."

"That seems to be the case," Raul replied walking toward his office window and looking out.

"They asked that I fill them in on what's going on with you and the Council. I suggested that I work with many world organizations and wasn't at liberty to discuss our confidential missions around the world."

"And?" Tyler replied.

"They noted that it would be very discouraging for the IRS to investigate the Council as to our non-profit status or for the FBI to release information about the activities they know we were involved in."

"So, they are threatening you to get your cooperation?"

"That's the way it looks," replied Raul as he returned to his desk. "However, I don't think they really know much about our activities nor do they have the contacts with the IRS or any creditable evidence that would show we are not operating as a non-profit organization."

Tyler decided he should take a look out the window. As he stood looking out many thoughts came to his mind. If Raul did tell them how they were related, then the FBI would obviously want to know much more about Tyler's powers. Then they could possibly declare him a national security risk and hold him for questioning. If Raul said he wouldn't cooperate and called their bluff, if it was a bluff, then they would continue to harass both of them. It looked like a lose-lose situation to Tyler.

"Then, I guess the best alternative would be for me to pick up their car tonight as they stake out my home and fly it to the Sahara and place them on a nice, warm sand dune," Tyler replied with a mischievous grin.

Raul turned and smiled as he realized that Tyler could see humor in the unpleasant situation. "I hadn't thought of that option, but why the Sahara?"

"I just figured they could use a vacation on a very large beach."

Now Raul couldn't help but laugh, as Tyler joined him.

"Anyway," Raul said, "this is a difficult choice. However, we too can play their game. Over the years I've helped a lot of important and influential people who would not like to see the World Disaster Relief Council injured in any way. I have a feeling that after a few phone calls I might be able to get agents Ferrell and Gerard transferred to that Sahara sand dune or at least pulled off their current assignment."

"That would be great," Tyler exclaimed. "Then what about the new world problems you wanted to discuss with me?"

"None of them are urgent, so we can hold that discussion until I'm sure we can get the FBI off our backs. Besides, if they decide to interrogate you, at this point, the less you know about the Council's activities, the better."

"Then I'm like on vacation from work for a few days?" Tyler asked.

Again, Raul laughed, "Something like that," he finally replied. "However, I did want to give you a heads up on one."

"I'm listening," replied Tyler.

"You know what a tsunami is and what it can do?"

"Sure, it's a massive series of waves caused by a large underwater earthquake in the ocean. It happens without warning and has devastated many shoreline countries over the years."

"That's right on, Tyler, and the biggest problem is that it happens, as you said, without warning so people affected don't have time to get to higher ground."

"And you think I can stop a tsunami?" Tyler questioned.

"Of course not, but when it happens you could be the fastest way for us to know how big the tsunami waves are and how fast and in what direction they are traveling. That way we could at least give the proper authorities the earliest information and save a lot of lives."

"I thought a world organization was placing ocean buoys all around the world to monitor unexpected waves during a tsunami."

"That is being done, but it's not complete. Even when it is complete those buoys are quite a-ways apart from each other and valuable time could be lost," replied Raul.

"Then my job would be to fly out to where the earthquake occurred and do a quick reconnaissance and let you know so you could contact the affected areas?"

"I can't believe you're only sixteen. You have the maturity of a much older person. Yes, that's exactly what I'd like you to be on call for. Are you willing to do that?" asked Raul.

"Of course, I'd be glad to, unless I'm in the middle of a test. I can't afford to get an 'F' in school. I hear you need top grades to get into Superhero College."

"With your mind telling you whatever you want to know, I'm sure you'll complete the test before the phone stops ringing," Raul replied.

"That's true, I almost forgot," Tyler said as he stood up. "Then let me know, that is, about the problem with the FBI as well as about any tsunamis that happen to pop up."

"That's a deal," Raul replied as they shook hands and Tyler headed towards the elevator.

Tyler took a taxi home, and when he arrived he saw Kensie and his cousins standing at the front door.

"Hey, Tyler!" Kensie shouted "Look who's going to the mall with us this morning."

Tyler was surprised. His mom, Christina, had mentioned that she was not working that day so maybe they would go to the mall for some things she needed. However, she'd said nothing about Nicholas, Jonathan, and Mikaia joining them.

"That sounds great to me. Raul just mentioned that I'm on a short vacation at least until school starts. But that's something else. Give me a moment to get ready while I make a quick call."

Tyler knew Raul had many important friends he could contact who might be able to get the FBI to back off, but Tyler wanted to be doubly sure they would.

"Hi Wake. This is Tyler. Sorry to bother you but I believe you could do something for me...you thought I might be calling...and you know about Agents Ferrell and Gerard's current inquiries?...Yes, I agree that their investigation could make things more difficult for all of us...Then you'll make a few calls to see what you can do? Great, thanks a lot."

Chapter Thirteen

A New Hero and Tsunami

"Okay Mom, you're the driver. We're off to the Westfield Century City Mall."

"The best women's stores are there, so of course," said Mikaia.

Kensie and Sydney agreed with her.

"Well, I guess you're almost women," stated Jonathan, "but I'd really like to go where all the girls are."

"I second the motion," interjected Nicholas.

A frustrated Mikaia turned to Jonathan and said, "Then why don't you go to the climbing tree in the children's play area. I'm sure you'll both find some girls there."

"That's not a bad idea but we'll have to wait a few years before we can ask any of them to the prom," mentioned Nicholas.

"Alright everyone," stated Christina. "I'm sure you three young men will find plenty to do there as well as see some young ladies parading about."

"Then as you four shop the three of us will head to the food court," said Tyler. "I could use a snack. Besides you never know who you'll find there."

"I'm game," added Jonathan.

"See, women think of clothing and guys think with their stomachs," replied Mikaia.

"Yeah, but at least we won't go hungry and we'll still have some pocket money left over. Then we'll head to the tree," he added with a smile.

"So, who have you saved since we saw you last at Disneyland?" asked Jonathan.

He took a bite of his hamburger and swallowed a couple of French fries at the same time.

"How about a freighter caught in a tropical storm south of Hawaii that was about to roll over," replied Tyler

"Wow!" stated Nicholas.

"And on the way back I took in the last half of a Dodgers baseball game."

"And you were just a few miles away from Waikiki, Hawaii," said Jonathan. "I would have dropped in there."

"I thought about that but then there was a massive tropical storm..."

"Oh, yeah. Then what else?" asked Jonathan.

"Well, I did help my friend Gary get his Dad's marine salvage boat unsnagged just off Santa Rosa Island."

"Why did you do that?" asked Nicholas.

"They were going to lose everything since the underwater winch was stuck and couldn't bring the gold up."

"Gold?" asked Jonathan as he choked on his third large bite of hamburger and began a fit of coughing.

"Yeah, a whole boatload of it from an 1850's sunken ship that was transporting if from the California goldfields to the east coast."

"Did you get to keep any of it or even touch it?" asked Nicholas.

"No, of course not! It would all belong to Gary's father who found it. I did get to pick up and place about a hundred pounds of gold bars into the scoop."

"Man I've never even seen a pound of gold before," stated Jonathan.

"Well, from several hundred dark feet underwater it didn't look too impressive. But yes, I would have liked a little as a souvenir."

"You need to get paid something for what you do," suggested Nicholas. "You risk your life and have saved hundreds of people and millions of dollars' worth of property."

"That's not why I do it. You know that. The deal is that while I'm living at home, I don't need the money.

When I'm on my own, and if I still have these powers, I will probably need some kind of salary from the Council."

"And that should be a big one I'd imagine," replied Jonathan.

"What do you mean, 'if I still have the powers'?" asked Nicholas.

"I still don't know how or why I was given all of them. I also don't know how long they'll last or if they will eventually turn on me, you know, burn me out or something."

"I see your point. For me, it's fun having a cousin who can do all these amazing things but I keep forgetting about all the stress you must have not knowing what exactly is going on," replied Nicholas.

"She can't breathe!" someone behind them yelled.

As the boys looked around, they noticed four college aged girls who were apparently having lunch at the table next to them. Two were standing up while one of them was holding her throat and halfway bent over. That girl kept gagging and her lips and face turned grayish from lack of oxygen. Everyone could see she was in distress.

Nicholas jumped up, ran over behind her, pulled her shoulders back to straighten her up a bit. Then he threw his arms around her lower chest and his fists together under her ribs. He pushed his fists quickly into her upper abdomen several times trying to use the air in her lungs to dislodge whatever was blocking her airway. On the fourth thrust upwards she coughed several times and started taking several quick breaths. She collapsed into her seat and after a moment or two was breathing deeply.

"Are you all right, Aubry?" her panicked friend yelled.

Aubry slowly nodded her head.

Her friend looked over at Nicholas. "You saved her. She could have died if someone hadn't done what you did!"

By then several people had gathered around her to make sure she was going to be all right. Jonathan and Tyler were also there.

"Great work, Nicholas," said Jonathan.

"Speaking of quick thinking and saving others, look what you just did," said Tyler, "the Heimlich Maneuver."

Aubry seemed more comfortable now but still looked scared. She stood up and gave Nicholas a hug.

"You saved me," she said softly. "Thank you, I thought I was going to die. It all happened so quickly."

Not knowing what to say, Nicholas replied, "You're welcome. I'm glad you're okay."

As the boys sat back down, Aubry, asked if they would join her friends and her at their table. An invitation from four attractive girls was quickly agreed to.

The boys found out that the four girls were students at UCLA. Aubry was from San Francisco and planned to finish her major in Biology and apply to medical school to become a Pediatrician. After a short time of visiting, Christina, Mikaia, Kensie, and Sydney appeared. Mikaia had this amazed expression on her face when she saw the boys sitting with several attractive older girls. She smiled as she approached and tried to figure out the situation.

Jonathan noticing her quandary said, "Hey, look who we met at the tree."

Tyler and Nicholas started laughing.

Aubry told them the story about how Nicholas had saved her from suffocating. Christina and the cousins were quite impressed. Nicholas just sat still and smiled.

After a few minutes of conversation, the boys all got hugs from Aubry. She saved the longest hug and kiss on the cheek for Nicholas.

The seven of them ended up at the yogurt shop.

"Now we have two heroes," said Christina, "so I'll pay for the yogurt."

Jonathan immediately put his smaller yogurt cup back down and began to fill the largest one he could find. The others all stared at him.

"So, Nicholas is a hero, and we have to celebrate that somehow," Tyler said as he took a large spoonful of chocolate mousse. "Besides, now there are two of us who we can refer to as 'greased lightening.'"

That night Tyler received a call from Raul who told him that the situation with agents Ferrell and Gerard was happening much faster than he expected. Apparently, the Agency had quickly evaluated their investigation of Tyler and the Council and found no basis to continue that investigation. The two agents were reassigned to investigate the theft of postage stamps at a post office near the Mexican border above Tijuana. Apparently, the agents were not pleased with their assignment.

Tyler couldn't help but smile. He knew he no longer had to be as careful as he'd been. Yet, he would miss the cream-colored car that seemed to show up everywhere he went.

Tyler thanked Raul for his call and let his parents and sisters know what had happened.

That night Tyler once more laid in bed staring out the window at the moon. He wondered if going to the moon would be his next adventure. After all, he had just recently flown one hundred and fifty miles into space at speeds exceeding 17,000 miles an hour. What else was there left for him to do? But how was this all possible? What did God have in mind for him?

Tyler soon dozed off. It was the first full night's sleep he'd had for a long time.

The next morning Tyler and his father, Matt, had a long talk about Tyler's powers and the resulting questions. Matt understood Tyler's concerns but of course had few answers that could comfort him. Matt told him that he should just continue doing what felt right to him, remember who he really was, and trust that in the right time God would give him the answers to his questions. Tyler hoped that those answers would come soon.

At noon, just as Tyler had picked up his golf clubs to go to the driving range, the phone rang.

"Tyler, its Raul," said his dad.

"Hi Raul, what's up?"

Tyler listened for a few minutes before replying, "You must be clairvoyant, Raul. You just told me about the possibility and now it's happened?... the Mariana Trench several hundred miles off the Philippine Coast?... What was the size of the earthquake? It's rated an 8? That can be very destructive, can't it? ...Yes, I'll be right over."

"Man, Dad, I thought I was on vacation. Now the one thing that gets me back happens. Would you drop me off at Raul's?"

"Sure. Are you in a big hurry?"

"You probably need to drive just a little faster than a tsunami."

"Then let's leave now!" Matt answered as they headed out the door.

When they met Raul, he said, "Okay, do you understand what you need to do, and do you have the GPS coordinates?"

"Approach the Philippines and follow west checking for any large waves that may threaten them. Next, turn around and go east to see if any were headed towards the western Pacific countries."

"Right, and if you see any problems call on the satellite phone I gave you. That way I can quickly notify the countries that may be threatened."

Tyler nodded as he jumped out of Raul's tenth story window and shot west towards the sun. He could feel its warmth as he climbed towards it. He was so energized that he figured he'd be off the Philippine coast in about twenty minutes.

Tyler smiled as he sped across the Pacific. A few weeks earlier he was an ordinary guy just enjoying his summer. Now he was off on another adventure with the possibility of saving thousands of people's lives. He wasn't even concerned about losing some vacation time. He was given these powers for a purpose so he had better do all he could to help while he was still able. Besides how many people have had the opportunity to change the position of a satellite by actually flying 150 miles up into space? He thought for a moment about how awesome that would sound on the six o'clock news. However, it was not all about him, but rather what he could do for others.

He kept a sharp eye on the ocean below as he headed west and looked for any possible large waves or turbulence caused by the earthquake. So far so good, he thought hoping he wouldn't find any.

Unfortunately, about five minutes off the coast of the Philippines he spotted a series of very large waves. The good news was that the largest ones were headed west towards South America. They had a long way to go and would likely soften or dissipate over the next several thousand miles. The waves rushing west towards the Philippines from the Marianna Trench earthquake, although smaller, could still cause some damage to lower coastal areas.

Tyler followed the smaller waves west and determined that at the speed they were going they would probably hit the coast in about four to five hours. He immediately called Raul and told him of his findings. Raul quickly notified his contacts in the Philippines who had been warning the people of a possible tsunami. Now they would order everyone to move swiftly to higher ground.

Then Tyler changed course and followed the larger waves east as they moved towards Central America and the countries of Columbia, Ecuador and Peru. As he followed them, Tyler figured they were traveling about four hundred to five hundred miles per hour and should reach the coast in about fourteen hours. Although the lead waves had decreased in height over the last several hundred miles, they might cause some damage when they arrived. Once again, Tyler called Raul and informed him of his findings and the approximate direction and speed of the waves.

Raul told Tyler to return to his office. After a few hours Tyler could make another pass over the west bound waves to determine how much they had slowed and possibly dissipated.

Tyler agreed and turned north for a leisurely flight along the South and Central American coasts as he headed back towards Los Angeles.

"Wow! What was that?" Tyler exclaimed. Within a few seconds Tyler's speed had dropped off dramatically and he'd plunged about a thousand feet. Although he was able to level off and even start to climb, he realized something was wrong. Except for when he was learning how to control his flying this was the first time he'd suddenly lost control. He felt his heart beat faster. What if he'd dropped all the way down? What could he do if he did lose control?

Many thoughts passed through his mind. He'd felt invincible until now. Did something momentarily block the sun's rays? Were his powers fading? Or was it just some kind of fluke that would never happen again? Tyler knew he had no one he could ask and that in itself worried him.

Tyler continued his flight but was more cautious. He slowed down his speed and lowered his height. It seemed to take forever before he dropped in through the office window that Raul had left open.

"Good job, Tyler," said Raul as he grabbed Tyler's hand and shook it.

Tyler was very glad to see Raul but wasn't sure what he should say to him about his mishap.

"Thanks, Raul. It was basically a routine trip for me. I hope the countries receiving the calls from you are able to alert everyone on time."

"They knew there would be a possible tsunami after such a large and deep ocean earthquake so they had everyone on alert ready to go. So, to answer your question, yes, thanks to you they had the time to notify just about everyone."

"Will you be able to take a quick trip back in a few hours to double check on the size and speed of the waves heading towards the South American Coast?

Tyler didn't answer at first. He'd almost forgotten that his task wasn't over. Did he want to fly back so soon? No. He just wasn't confident in his powers any more. He did know that he couldn't say "no" to Raul without giving him a reason. Did he want to tell him about his loss of power? Probably not, at least until he had a chance to gather some information.

"Yeah, sure, just let me know. I'll be in the back office you let me use."

Chapter Fourteen

Seeking Answers

Tyler needed to find a reason for his power loss before he would feel comfortable enough to fly. He knew he wasn't flying in clouds when he fell so that was out. The next thing that crossed his mind was that it could have been a solar or lunar eclipse, but then that only happened a couple times each year and he would have been in darkness when he fell which he wasn't.

He kept searching for answers. He considered a massive daytime storm or shower of meteors or shooting stars. Maybe one of these happened and caused the shadows that instantly blocked the sun. He wouldn't have noticed except for the loss of his power source. Yeah, that may have happened. After all it did just affect him for a few seconds. Tyler quickly checked and discovered that there was currently a large meteor shower taking place that he would be able to see in the evening.

Tyler felt that the meteor shower could have been the culprit. This eased his mind a bit. However, the shower was still going on and he wondered if it would affect his return trip to the South American coast.

After eating a quick lunch that Raul had brought back to the office for him, Tyler was on his way again. He knew that many people were counting on him so at this point what else could he do?

Tyler jumped out the window with some trepidation and quickly lifted towards the sun at a great speed. As he turned south, he was encouraged by the power and response he felt in his body and mind. He blanked out any negative thoughts and concentrated on the tsunami, finding the waves and then reporting. The coastal towns and cities were depending on him.

Soon he spotted the waves about two thousand miles off shore or about five hours away. They had slowed and also decreased in size but by landfall they still would be a force to contend with. He used the satellite phone and reported to Raul. Raul immediately called his contacts. Tyler knew there was nothing else he could do. There was no way he could stop or lessen a tsunami's force. It would hit the northern five to six hundred miles of the South American coast. The people had been hit before and would be doing all they could to lessen any loss of life or property.

Tyler had just started back home when his flight was disrupted again. It didn't happen all at once but incrementally. He began to slow down and lose altitude. He encouraged his body to move faster but it was as though the sun was setting when it wasn't. He knew he needed to concentrate and focus on his flight and on his light source, the sun. He continued but it was a battle of wills, his against whatever it was that was interrupting his power. Was this his kryptonite? What was causing his lack of control?

Soon he was through Raul's open window and dropping into a chair, physically and mentally exhausted.

Tyler took a cab home again. He thought how nice it would be if his parents actually bought another car that he and eventually his sisters could use. He knew that this flying business wasn't practical for everyday life activities, especially if his goal was to keep his powers a secret.

Tyler's parents were all ears. They knew he was dealing with the Marianna Trench earthquake and wanted to know all about his adventure. Tyler really didn't feel like talking. He was still concerned about his power failures. However, he had told himself that he'd always keep them informed about his activities. He needed their understanding and support. So, he gave them the complete story, except the part that worried him the most.

After dinner there was a knock at their door. Tyler was nearby so he checked it. In front of him was a tall man in a suit. It was Brace, Wake's assistant. Tyler stepped back, surprised that Brace would actually be at his front door.

"Who is it?" asked his Mom.

"Oh, just someone from Raul's office giving me some information I requested," he answered.

Tyler didn't want to mislead his mom, but he also didn't want to worry her either. His parents still weren't sure about his and Wake's relationship, or what Wake's real intentions were.

"Brace," Tyler muttered, "what can I do for you?"

"Sorry to have to approach you at home but Wake needs to meet with you as soon as possible.

Tyler thought for a moment before answering.

"Then how about first thing tomorrow morning?"

Brace didn't smile.

"He wants to meet with you now. There is something he needs to tell you that's very important. He's right outside waiting in the limo."

Tyler was both curious and concerned.

"Mom and Dad, I need a few minutes to get something from his car. I'll be right back."

He followed Brace down the stairs and found the limo parked on the side street just around the corner.

"Tyler, please come in," Wake said and then he rolled back up his window.

Brace opened the door so Tyler could slide into the back seat next to Wake.

"You are probably quite tired by now, Tyler. You've had a difficult day. I'm sorry I need to bother you but I think this conversation will help you understand many things."

Tyler knew Wake well enough by now to feel a little more comfortable in his presence.

"Then how can I help you and what is this important thing you need to tell me?"

"I haven't been completely honest with you. I didn't know how you'd handle all of this, but now I've gotten to know you better and understand you. You have my admiration for what you can do and how you do it."

"I appreciate that but what do you want to tell me?"

"Let me get right to the point. Do you know where your power comes from?"

"I get my power from light, especially the sun. I seem to function like a large solar cell absorbing the light and then use its power to do amazing things. But I thought you knew that already."

"I actually knew it before you did."

Tyler wasn't sure what Wake meant by that and thought for a moment how he'd respond.

"I was aware that you know just about everything that happens to me, but how could you know about my source of power before I did?"

Wake paused for a moment while looking directly at Tyler responded, "Because I am the one who gave you that power."

Tyler gasped.

"You what? You gave me my power?"

"Yes."

"I can't believe it. How could you...?"

Wake interrupted,

"Just a moment, and I'll explain. Today, while you were flying back and forth to the tsunami didn't you lose some of your power?"

Tyler couldn't believe that Wake would know about that. He hadn't even mentioned it to his parents or Raul.

"Yes, that did happen to me. How did you know?"

"Because I monitor your every move."

Now Tyler was a little scared.

"Why do you do that?"

"Because you are actually my creation...although I don't want it to sound like I own you or anything."

"How do you figure that?"

"I'm sure that you and Raul checked me out and know I own a company named Great Minds International. We help companies solve problems that make them more efficient and help them develop new ways of doing things. Many of the companies we help are in the bio tech and thermodynamic world. This is partly because I have a Doctorate degree in Molecular Biology with research in thermodynamics.

You put those two areas together the right way and you have, let's say, you."

"But you didn't even know me. How did you choose me?"

"Our main research center is near the Los Angeles Airport, but I have an auxiliary office in Redondo near the beach. I've spent a lot of time walking along the bluff above that beach over the last year. I've watched a lot of young people as they interacted with others. I've seen you with your parents and sisters several times and with your three cousins also. You impressed me. You were athletic and active, yet helpful and friendly. You seemed to want to make others happy and do what was right. All those would be great traits for a superhero."

"Then you picked me for your experiment?"

"Something like that. Actually, you helped me save the powers you've been given."

"I what?"

"You flew up to and saved the satellite I had previously launched. That satellite not only helps ships navigate but is the basis for your powers. One of the reasons you received these powers when you did was so you could save the satellite."

Tyler's mind was spinning. Every time Wake gave him information, he wanted more. Wake chose him on the beach and gave him satellite activated super powers?

"I know what light power can do, so am I just a big solar cell?" Tyler asked.

Wake smiled.

It was the first time Tyler had seen him do that.

"Partly, you do absorb light and get much of your energy from it, but there is much more. It has to do with DNA sequencing and something called Single Nucleotide Polymorphism or SNP'S. Our satellite focuses on you and makes adjustments all the time. We have learned to do a variety of adjustments that have a great effect on many of your body's functions. Most adjustments will be with you forever. Others will be more limited. For instance, today when you lost some control these continuing adjustments were momentarily lost due to the static caused by a massive meteorite storm. You should be fine except occasionally when something like this happens."

Tyler thought about what Wake had said. He understood some of the science Wake said went into his "adjustments."

"Then can these powers I have be turned off?" he finally asked.

"No, most of them are now part of you. They may help you have a longer life since you will always be in good mental and physical condition, but eventually you will age like everyone else. You are superhuman, but you are still human."

"This is all so hard to believe. I have a lot of adjustments myself to make."

"So far you have made me and my researchers very proud. The way you have helped and saved people while not drawing attention to yourself, makes us all realize we have chosen the right person," said Wade as he reached over and shook Tyler's hand.

"Then what's next?" asked Tyler.

"Just be yourself as we support you and we both learn from what you do. You are sort of a research project for us, a very important one. We have no desire to control you besides making a few occasional adjustments to keep your powers up to date."

Tyler was excited and worried at the same time. Now he knew the source of his powers and why he had them. He knew he would have these powers throughout his life with some slight unknown adjustments. He was a human being who had been altered to receive his superhuman powers from light. Yet, he had had no choice in this experiment. What if he didn't want to be superhuman? But then again, if he had been given a chance to choose, wouldn't he have chosen to do so anyway? There were still some things he needed to understand, but for now even though he didn't choose this life, somehow, he felt free.

As Tyler thought about the previous weeks, he couldn't help but smile. Kensie had been right. Every superhero has his Kryptonite and his, apparently, was Wake.

Epilogue

After talking to Wake, Tyler hurried back into his house. He couldn't believe what he'd just been told, yet, at the same time, it finally all made sense.

Tyler spent most of the evening explaining to his family the information he'd been given by Wake. Now he knew that he wasn't sick, or abnormal, or crazy. He was a planned project who was monitored and watched over, but not controlled, by Wake and his researchers.

He told his family how his powers had been interrupted by a massive meteorite storm as he followed the tsunami, but his powers returned quickly due to adjustments by Wake's researchers.

"Who is this Wake, really?" asked his Dad. "And what do you mean, you're a 'planned project?'"

"Actually, Wake watched me on Redondo Beach and picked me out of everyone to be in his project. He has a company called Great Minds International which deals with research in bio tech and thermodynamics, areas in which he has a Doctoral Degree."

"Is this something you really want to be a part of?" asked his mom.

"I've thought a lot about this over the last couple of weeks. If he had asked me, I probably would have said, 'Yes,' anyway. I don't think I would have passed up a chance to have super powers with which I could help so many people...look at all I've been able to do!"

"I'm glad you finally have the answers you've been searching for," said Kensie. "And I'm really glad you're my brother even though you can outrun me and everything else."

"Okay," said his Dad, "now is a good time to tell you about the gift your mom and I have decided to give you. You have really earned it."

"It's not my birthday or anything is it?" Tyler asked.

"No," replied his mom, "but if you're going to keep doing this superhero stuff as Energized Man, you're going to need some practical way to get around town that doesn't involve flying."

"You mean..." Tyler started to say.

"Yes, you now have a new silver Subaru Crosstrek," said his Dad. "Raul wanted to kick in a little too."

"Really! Thank you!" shouted Tyler. "This will really help me!"

"Now when Kensie starts to drive in a couple of years," said his mom, "we hope you'll share it some with her. We only have so many parking spaces."

"I like that idea," said an enthusiastic Kensie. "You know we have our final Planning Committee meeting to welcome the new Freshmen tomorrow. You can drive us there!"

"It will be my pleasure!" replied an excited Tyler. "Can we see the car now?"

"Sure," said his Dad. "We have it in a special parking spot under the building."

The next morning Tyler couldn't wait to go down to see his new car. Even though he had taken his family for a short drive the night before, he hadn't had a chance to check out all its features. He had spent part of the evening reading through the long Owner's Manual.

"Tyler!" Kensie yelled. "Remember, our meeting is this morning, so don't go too far if you mean to take another test drive."

"Okay, I'll be right back."

An hour later, Tyler and Kensie pulled up in front of their high school. Tyler hoped some of his friends would be around to see his new car.

"Darn it! I wish it were a school day so I could sort of show off my new car. Don't see anyone but that girl on the stairs."

"Oh, her," replied Kensie. "She's a new girl who Sally brought to the first meeting we had. You know, the one you missed. She's going to help too. Sally thought that would be a good way for her to start meeting people."

As Tyler headed to the school meeting room, he saw the new girl standing by the door.

"Hi," Tyler said as he pulled the door open for her. "I'm Tyler, and who are you?"

"Oh, Hi. I'm April, nice to meet you."

Tyler paused for a moment. He sensed a confidence in her voice that he found attractive. He knew he had to find out more about her.

"Where are you coming from?"

"Oh, my family and I just moved here from Redondo a few weeks ago for my Junior year," she replied smiling.

"That's a coincidence," Tyler said. "Redondo, that's my favorite beach."

"I just lived two blocks from the beach and spent a lot of time there."

"That's great," Tyler replied. "I spend as much time there as I can, if I'm not busy working."

"What do you do for summer work?" April asked.

Tyler wasn't sure what he should say since he knew he couldn't say much.

"When I'm needed, I help out a couple of business men in town."

"I've lived in L.A. all my life," April replied. "I may know them."

"I don't think so, but one is named Raul and the other is named Wake."

April's eyes lit up.

"I don't know any business man named Raul but I do know a businessman named Wake quite well. He has an office in the Redondo area."

"You do?" A surprised Tyler asked.

April paused for a moment before she replied, "Yes, I do a little work for him off and on, too. He calls me 'Sunshine.'"

With that, Tyler wasn't sure what to say.